August, 197_

To the Bread Loaf Writers

from

Connie Brandhoff

PARTY PARTY

GIRL-FRIENDS

two short novels by
Ronni Sandroff

Alfred · A · Knopf   New York   1975

PARTY PARTY

GIRL-FRIENDS

This is a Borzoi Book
Published by Alfred A. Knopf, Inc.

Grateful acknowledgment is made to Tee Pee Music Co.,
Inc., for permission to reprint the lyrics on page 27
by W. D. Williams from the song sung by Ray Charles
entitled "Crying Time"; and to Project Seven Music
for permission to reprint the lyrics on page 89 from
"The Stranger Song," by Leonard Cohen.
Copyright © 1966 by Project Seven Music,
division of C.T.M.P., Inc., New York, New York.

Library of Congress Cataloging in Publication Data
Sandroff, Ronni.   Party party and Girlfriends.
    I. Title. II. Title: Girlfriends.
PZ4.S213Par   [PS3569.A5196]   813'.5'4   74-21337
ISBN 0-394-49494-6

Manufactured in the United States of America
First Edition

*This book is dedicated
to my friends from Iowa City and Maine,
who know why, and to my parents,
Sylvia and Michael Sandroff,
for always reminding me
I like to write.*

PARTY
PARTY

"*The purpose of man is to create more and more consciousness.*"
—Carl Jung

"*To be too acutely conscious is a disease.*"
 —Fyodor Dostoyevsky

1

Ever since I was old enough to measure my penis I was looking for a girl like Allegra. The kind you see on movie posters: polished bellies laced in blood. Allegra's chalky throat is beautiful enough to slit. Grabbed from behind on a foggy night in London by a thin strangle of string. Speared in the belly by a rampaging ape. What do you say? Throat-cutting or belly-spearing? Eyeball-slicing? What a sensuous corpse she'd make.

Well, what am I supposed to say? It's only a matter of minutes before I get maudlin again. You're the one who's trying to push me out into the cold night. Shall I act? How shall I act? Murder is all I can think of at the moment: divorce would be too mild a gesture. It's after midnight, for God's sake. She's been gone over eight hours now! If she had the consideration to disappear on schedule it would relieve the suspense. But there's no regularity. In September it was four nights in a row and then not again for a month, two months, and just as I was regaining that smug attitude that most marriages relax on, she doesn't meet me after class and I'm stuck with a carful of clean laundry and no wife to put the sheets on the bed.

The laundry thing enrages me most at the moment. I would like to go to bed. I want to leave your crummy apartment for my own crummy apartment and go to sleep. But she laundered the sheets before class this morning and the mattress is a naked, buttoned, gray-striped sponge of despair. If Allegra were here she'd put a deep blue sheet on the bed. In the dark I can feel the blueness of the sheet under my palms: coarse, cool blueness, so much more humane than white. Alas—no Allegra. Only sympathetic, sardonic brother Roger.

The topic for tonight, brother, is my marriage, my wife and myself. You look so sleepy. One man's marriage is not insignificant. But you go right to sleep and I'll just keep talking and if I say anything worth repeating I'll wake you up and repeat it. That's much better—the look of forced attention. I do my best to repress things but they all come spewing out. I can't think except by talking; whenever my mouth is shut my mind is blank—and sometimes when my mouth is going.

We have to get the history down first. Before you dare to tell me to act you have to know all the facts, the whole history of being Allegra. We have all night for metaphysics and theology and the rest of the college catalogue. First the facts, with all their multiple interpretations.

Allegra—earth mother, vestal virgin, bitch goddess, golden fleece, daughter of the dry east wind. Laughing, giggling, prancing, whoring Allegra. Right now, stone drunk, in someone else's bed.

Her childhood doesn't interest me. She was knock-hockey champion at the local playground, won a science-fair competition, wore red rubbers when it rained. Nothing ever happens before adolescence, and nothing really happens after. Sometime during her eleventh year her eyes wandered past the comic books to confession and pin-up magazines. She chucked dreams of being a buccaneer pirate, a princess, a mommy. She became a rebel: she wanted to be the kind of girl her mother wouldn't let her play with. She wanted to be a mammoth-breasted beauty strutting across magazine covers in spike-heeled shoes. She gorged herself on stories about the starlet and the producer, wife-trading suburbia, drunken step-fathers, breast surgery, and exactly what happened at the drive-in on prom night in Storm Lake, Minnesota. She invented a place called Derby (after the peanut butter brand) where sex and violence reigned. The sleek-legged women were submissive slaves to the men who could grab any woman they wanted, feel her up, undress her, lay her right there in the gutter. Allegra estimated she had this fantasy for fifteen hours a day for two years.

She must have glared out at the world a few minutes a day, because when she was eleven and a half she started fol-lowing around a group of neighborhood girls who called themselves the She-Cats. The first important day in her life was a visit to the Paradise Movie House. The Paradise is impressive to a kid, damn impressive. It's the largest movie house in the Bronx, the tallest and gaudiest in the world. She was only eleven. Her grandparents had taken her there once as a birthday treat. Now she was going on Saturday after-noon and she was with the She-Cats: Cookie! Candy! Joanie! Sandy! and Fluffy! Fluffy, can you imagine? Her real name was Martha or something. Allegra chants those names like a charm to dispel the Mortimers who surround her now. Cookie candy joanie sandy and fluffy. Always like that, with Fluffy set off as a particularly delectable tidbit. They sang this to the bus driver:

I wish I was a fascinating lady
My past would be dark, my future would be shady
I'd live in a house with a little red light
I'd sleep all day and I'd work all night
And once a month, I'd take a short vacation
And drive my customers wild!
I wish I was a fascinating lady
Instead of a delinquent child.

Cookie was her best friend. She dyed her hair yellow and wore a black cardigan buttoned down the back to show off her bust. When the Paradise manager patted Cookie's ass she screamed, "Molest, molest!" Allegra was eleven and these girls were thirteen and smoked cigarettes and wore baby-poo-pink lipstick all over their teeth. And they had pimples. Allegra felt very left out that year.

She didn't have pimples or the pink calamine stuff to spread all over them. She followed the She-Cats to the Paradise with her chest bursting. Three or four hundred teenagers stood in the lobby throwing popcorn at the huge goldfish hiding under the waterfalls. They passed a police-man, and the She-Cats, in one motion, covered their faces. Allegra was left staring right at him. An embarrassing ad-mission: she wasn't afraid of cops. They waited on the first landing, rubbing their fingers against red velvet, waiting until the matron went to check on some screams coming from the bathroom, then dashed up the flight of purple stairs to the balcony. You have to be sixteen to sit in the balcony.

Above the balcony there's a night-blue dome sparkling with stars, a yellow moon, clouds moving through the mist, cupids darting through the clouds. In the alcoves on the walls they have these pseudo-Greek statues with lavender lights illuminating naked couples coupling. Paradise. Allegra could hardly breathe. The screen lit up. The She-Cats blew smoke rings into the beams. Cookie. Candy. Joanie. Sandy. Fluffy. And Allegra watching the couple in front of her twist their heads as they kissed so they could see the screen.

The matron came down the aisle but didn't notice them. They giggled, sat on their feet, smoked, spun their heads to get a look at the boys. Cookie got picked up first in her black black sweater. An usher shone his light in her face, down her body; Cookie followed him to the make-out section. Ushers are status in a movie house, like lifeguards around a pool. Anyone official in a uniform. It sets them apart from the jerks in sport shirts. An usher in maroon pants. Allegra gets scared. She pictures the She-Cats leaving one by one. She's young, her hair is natural red, she wears the smallest bra they make.

Joanie and Fluffy marched off with two boys from Clinton High School. Sandy met a guy she picked up in the zoo a few months before and they don't bother going off, they make out right there under Allegra's nose. She watched the picture. She hummed "Earth Angel." She pulled the stuffing out of her seat. Then a cigarette lighter flashed near her hair. A boy climbed over the row to sit next to her. "What's your name?" "Allegra." "Allegra?" (She got that all the time.) "Yeah." "Yeah. My name's Tony." Allegra was ecstatic. Tony is the best name in the world, all her fantasies were populated with men named Tony. "I just love the name Tony." He stood up. "Let's go sit on the side."

She followed him up the aisle and over. He walked in front of her, never saying a word. They passed Cookie playing with the flashlight on the usher's lap. They edged down an empty row, sitting next to the night-blue wall under a naked statue. He kissed her, ramming her side into the arm rest, a long kiss right through the rest of the picture, the intermission, the next feature, a newsreel. He grabbed at her breast a few times and she let him, but pulled away when he put her hand on his crotch. It's a long, wet, languid kiss. She's transported—a transcendental experience. Passion and personality don't exist. She looked up at the alabaster cupid, thinking, "Tony," and it was the name that counted; she had no curiosity about him. She wasn't self-conscious or afraid; she transcended everything, focusing her existence on his lips and hers and the naked Greek above them. During the whole time she never questioned the morality, never doubted that she was loving right then and would stop loving as soon as the movie was over, that it would be a complete, whole thing without repercussions, emotions, sexuality. She lost her identity in his thick lips and the taste of her own lipstick. It was perfect. When the movie ended she wiped her mouth, waved goodbye, and ran to tell her friends that his name was Tony.

I get in a sweat when I think about that guy Tony. I'm more jealous of him than I'll ever be of the guy she's sleeping with tonight. Tony gave her something mindless, whole, a rounded memory. All the guy tonight will give her is a squirt of sperm.

She never went back to the Paradise. She had had "it." After that she became reckless. She cut school, roaming around Greenwich Village, Central Park, Times Square movie houses, laughing when the perverts tried to pick her up, letting them put their hands under her skirt, laughing when even the She-Cats were shocked. You see, those girls had rules. Sexual activity was coded from one to nine, a system which filtered down from some sociological survey. It was good to know the code because then you could talk on the phone with mother at your elbow. Here it is, Roger, in case you ever have little girls to cope with:

#1: kissing
#2: feeling on top, over clothes
#3: feeling on top, under clothes
#4: feeling on bottom, over clothes
#5: feeling on bottom, under clothes
#6: feeling him, over clothes
#7: feeling him, under clothes
#8: almost
#9: all the way!

Allegra never bought the system. First of all, she did things that weren't listed. The She-Cats never went further than number two on a pick-up. But, if your mother was out of town for the weekend, thought Allegra, why miss the opportunity? Of course she was affected by the system. The other girls talked about getting so hot they could barely manage to keep their limits. Allegra thought she was some kind of a sex maniac, and she was still thinking that when I met her. But she's wrong. She doesn't have any more sexual impulses than other women; she just interprets every sensation as sexual. If her scalp tingles when she brushes her hair or her skin puckers in the bath—she thinks it's all sex. Fear, anger, pain, gargling. When we were first married we experimented for a while; every time she had a sensation we went to bed, and of course she wasn't ready most of the time.

Anyway, by the time Allegra was fourteen she tired of pick-ups. The thrill blew away on a drafty subway platform. She had really been alone all those years. The gang kids she spent summer evenings with weren't like her. They were sure of their rules. It was all right to rip the seats on the subways but taboo to curse your mother. If a girl didn't have limits she was a dirty little who-ah. Allegra didn't have the same limits for all guys. If she was with a man in his twenties she tried to do what he expected. If she was with a high-school kid, well, she didn't want to be his teacher. I'm the only man Allegra has ever condescended to teach.

In high school she moved from the She-Cats to the Misfits. Every group Allegra has ever associated with has a name. The Misfits were five sixteen-year-old Jewish boys with high IQs, communist parents, unrepressed childhoods, and unimpaired virginity. These kids were out to refute all systems, including time, language, being, and nothingness. Allegra said when she first met them they treated her like Wendy in *Peter Pan*: at last we have a mother, at last we have a mother.

The most important Misfit to her was Morris because his wonderful house was usually free of parents. Morris lived in a peaked two-story house set way back from the street by an overgrown garden. It stood between the twelve-story apartment buildings which seemed to lean over it and discuss its doom. Allegra knew the house before she knew Morris. Then one day, there was Morris in a dark blue sweatshirt and loose pants, staring, opening the gate, waving her in.

Inside, the Misfit circus was going on. Five shoeless boys slouched over the furniture smoking cigarettes. The record player spun Bach and rock-and-roll alternately. The ashtrays filled and filled until they spilled over on the floor. It looked strange to Allegra. The boys she knew wore tight pants and tried to look as tough as possible. The Misfits cultivated the shnook look. She walked into their lives, sat down, and stayed for several years.

The Misfits' main occupation was smoking. It was not merely a habit, it was an organized pastime, a ritual, a method of telling time. No one ever came to Morris's house without several packs of cigarettes. His parents had large modern-art ashtrays all over the house. They slouched, smoking one cigarette after another, flipping the ashes over each other, crushing the butts into all the other butts in the ashtray, trading brands, eating the tobacco, scribbling messages on empty packs and throwing them at each other, peeling the butts open, and blowing on the ashes. Allegra was the only one who smoked filters, so her cigarette butts were a star attraction. They played snap-the-filter, peel-the-filter, save-the-filter. Allegra says she had to smoke faster and faster to keep up with the demand for filters. After two to three packs in an afternoon she would get dizzy and pass out on Morris's bed as if drunk.

One of the boys would follow her into the bedroom and fall down next to her; soon all five of them would be lying on Morris's single bed trying to figure out what to do with Allegra. Biting was a popular occupation. Allegra would sink her teeth into Gary's forearm, biting as hard as she could until he pulled her hair, the signal for "I give." Then he bit her thigh, right through skirt and stockings, waiting for the signal from her. Then the other boys would join in until five of them bit the victim at once. When they got too sore to bite,

Morris would try to swallow Allegra's breast. The group had a remarkably long attention span. Every small activity they dreamed up was practiced for hours and hours.

They didn't always stay at Morris's house. As a matter of fact they were always trying to leave it. "Let's go for a ride on the subway," someone would say, and someone would agree, but with a twist of the wrist which meant, "as soon as I finish my cigarette." Of course, by the time his cigarette was finished, someone else had lit one. A rather unique inertia mechanism, I think. When they finally did get onto the subway they made complete fools of themselves. Allegra was used to the kind of kids who would do anything to be ignored and start a fight if anyone stared at them. But the Misfits invited stares and backed off from fights. They played statues on the subway. One boy would make his face and body pliable while another sculpted an expression and position on him. Silly things—glasses on upside-down, tongue hanging out, eyes crossed, fingers pointing in ten directions, legs and arms crazily interwoven, cheeks in a grin.

Allegra adapted herself to the group. She no longer wore sexy, male-attracting clothes; she seldom brushed her hair; she threw away her cosmetic collection. She was boldly ridiculous in sloppy shirts, children's mittens, snow boots. She has a few pictures from those days: funny shots with five boys piled on top of her, all with their glasses on upside-down. She looks radiant in her sloppiness. I think she was happy with them. The boys stuck together because they had no friends or girlfriends among more stable kids, because they didn't know what to do with their time or energy, because they felt sexually inferior and intellectually superior to every human being on earth. But she, she was . . . "I was just one of them," she says, but I don't believe it. I'm sure she was idolized, coveted, the center of attention.

Her schoolwork vaulted into the superior zone as she began to compete a little with the boys. She loved history, arguing with the teachers, using radical lines culled from the Misfits. The teachers were snowed: they assumed the radicalism would pass; her reasoning power was fantastic; she was known to speak her mind in those days. They labeled her college material and put her in coach courses for the college boards over her father's objections. "My wife and I are not very smart," he told the guidance counselor, "so we would like the girl to learn something useful." She entered essay contests, did some debating, was elected into Arista. In her senior year she won a full scholarship to Sarah Lawrence.

Yeah yeah yeah, Roger, we're getting to the good part soon. You know I can't stand skipping anything. When Allegra got the scholarship notice in the mail she had a nervous breakdown that lasted for eight months until I met her and pulled her out of it. She did o.k. in college. She acquired a most conventional wardrobe, remnants of which still plague me. She traveled the ivy social circuit and ended up dating several of our fraternity brothers . . . of course you were such a big man then, Roger, you would never go out with a mere freshman. You were seeing that showy drama student who, whenever you deigned to say a word to her, said, "You know, Roger, I agree with you completely." But what essentially happened, what was going on in Allegra's mind now that she had lost Derby and the Misfits, is a mystery.

Bear with me, Roger! Don't you want to hear how I met her? All right now? All right. Let's see. The first time I saw Allegra, right, was in the New York apartment of three of our Amherst buddies. I had dropped college for a year—you remember—scholarship or no, I wanted out. Mother nagged and flagellated herself, but I went to New York. I was going to get a job, an apartment, and a loose Village chick to screw. I went to visit these fraternity brothers to find out about the "in" scene. Bright young executives in the making. Joe, Jack, and Mel or some such. Maybe Eddie or Johnny. It's too late to remember their names. Shit, Roger. When Allegra comes home you can ask her their names. I was sitting in their apartment, drinking, and this thing crawls out of the bedroom. Her hair was a red bird's nest, her clothes were filthy. her eyes blood-lined and swollen from crying. She crawled up to me, clawing the floor. Eddie threw a pack of cigarettes at her and told her to go back to bed. "What's that?" I asked. "That's an Allegra, vilest whore in New York." She rested her head on my knee. "I'm hungry," she said sadly.

"Take her off our hands if you want," Jack said. Now, I was a sensitive kid. In fact I still am a sensitive kid; it's a good role and I'm good at it. I felt bad for Allegra. Maybe she was alcoholic or psychotic. She was certainly better looking than Mel, John, and Eddie. I took her out for a cup of coffee. She had been on a real binge, the kind I thought only alcoholics could have. She hadn't been sober for two weeks, hadn't eaten, hadn't slept except when she passed out, which wasn't often. You know Allegra's capacity for alcohol.

So I took her out for coffee, took her to my room, washed her face, brushed her hair—she was beginning to look pretty—and fell in love with her. You have to put yourself in my position. Love was a dramatic sensation; it had to be aroused by an unusual woman, not some pale-eyed girl from Rhode Island. Allegra snuck in and out of my room in a downtown boarding house for three weeks. She was a good pal. We drank Thunderbird and other cheap brands. We talked and talked. Most of the things I've learned about her adolescence she told me then. We made plans. We would jump off the Staten Island ferry together. We would simultaneously slit each other's wrists. We would stow away on a Caribbean freighter and find ourselves an island with a cigarette machine all to ourselves.

She slept next to me most nights. I tucked the cover around her, arranged her hair on the pillow. I was afraid if I asked for sex I would be sucked into her corruption. My experience with women was limited to elaborately schemed pass attempts that failed out of their own elaboration. She was sure I respected her too much to screw her and began to love me out of sheer amazement, while I was sure the only thing I didn't feel was respect and began to love her for that. Something like that. We kept waking up and finding ourselves in love.

The tension was getting absurd for me. I wanted her body, but I didn't want the corruption. One night Allegra met me in front of my rooming house with a suitcase and four bottles of Thunderbird. We drove off to Maryland for a quick marriage. Tearing along the miles of well-lit highways, gas stations, telephone poles, my mind pushed through my drunkenness and I began to scare. I mean, Allegra wasn't the kind of girl I was brought up to expect to marry. She wasn't a virgin; that's the thought that kept running through my mind. I forgot about the millions of guys, her hatred of life . . . she wasn't a virgin.

"Sure you want to go through with this, Leggie?"

She was driving at the time. The car swerved. "Wasn't it your idea, Danny?"

"You're not a virgin."

"I never was a virgin," she said. "I was born wide open and ready. I was never deflowered. Honest. The first time was without pain, without blood."

That seemed to settle the question. It wasn't as if someone else had enjoyed her virginity. The thought excited me. She was born absolutely corrupt. No, not corrupt, but without innocence. Allegra isn't one of those hapless females who gets corrupted by her environment. On the contrary—she corrupts her environment, her friends. She is the source of evil, you see, and a mindless source. She didn't have any guilt then. I taught her that.

We decided to stop for gas and coffee. Allegra turned off the highway into the gas station. She didn't slow down. Her foot wasn't even over the brake. We hit a concrete-bordered flower bed at sixty miles an hour. "Ooops," she said as she was flung back on the plastic seat. The axle of the car was broken in two. I haven't let her drive since that day.

"This is a bad omen," Allegra said. "Maybe we should just live together." I sighed, drinking vending-machine coffee. We worked it out rationally. I would get a job, finally, and give up the rooming-house mess. She would get a job, a psychiatrist, and with my help straighten herself out. We'd live together, as if married, and get married when we really felt like it. We hugged each other. We hugged the vending machine. We hugged the water fountain.

I made Allegra call her mother, at two a.m., from Maryland and tell her our decision. Her mother cried, shocked at being woken up. "Do what you want. You always do. Why did you bother calling? You never call."

Of course I had talked her into calling. I wanted to call my parents, to play everything straight with them like they always told me to. There was also this small matter of a broken axle, would they mind wiring a hundred dollars? I placed the call to New Hampshire. I woke my mother up. She didn't cry. She was silent while I talked and talked. She was silent when I was finished, breathing heavily, begging her to respond. "Yes, well, it takes me a moment to collect my thoughts. Your father will wire the money in the morning. Isn't that a lovely thought, in the morning. If you love Allegra, we think you should marry her. You cannot live as man and wife without the sanction of God. It would never work. It would come out later and spoil your record."

I gave in instantly. I didn't mind taking my life . . . but to spoil my record? Allegra called her mother back and told her the new plan. Allegra's mother has soft, shrugging shoulders. She agreed. She'd make a wedding. She'd buy the gown. Couldn't they discuss it in the morning?

My mother is not the indulgent type. She's tough, uncompromising. Oh, I know you like her, Roger, and she likes you, as all mothers do. I remember the night you spent hours telling her how lucky you were to have a brilliant, loyal friend like me; and she told you how much she appreciated your good influence on me. She gets along with anyone who agrees with her, but can you imagine rebelling against her? She worshipped my brother and I as she ruled us, so we came to feel that only by obeying her could we become all the great things she told us we were.

I did my best to disguise Allegra. I bought her a navy spring suit with white trim, sent her to the beauty parlor, sobered her up. But as she stumbled into the upright New England living room in yo-yo-eyed fascination, my mother's skin turned gray. My father fell in love with her. "She's sparkling—she lives!"

My mother took Allegra into the white-and-pine Americana kitchen and started popping questions. What did Allegra think of me dropping school? Did she realize I had a fantastic intellectual potential? Did she realize it was absolutely essential that I return to Amherst and then go to graduate school? Yes, graduate school. Well, perhaps a year off in Europe for good behavior in between universities. Ocean-liner tickets always make a good graduation present. And what political party did Allegra favor? Did she realize I had a gift for politics? One of America's gravest problems was that its most brilliant men disdained public service. And God, did we realize how important He would be in helping us fulfill all our dreams?

Allegra said "Uh-huh." And "Huh?" She was not prepared for a predatory mother. She thought of mothers as soft things that cried and cleaned a great deal. My mother stuck fast to Allegra. She never confronted me or tried to change my mind about the marriage. How I longed to be confronted, to be talked out of it. Mother assumed I was unalterably convinced. Her only hope was to save us as a couple, to convince Allegra that I was little Thomas Jefferson to be coddled, coaxed, and shoved back to school. The more inevitable the marriage became the more frantic I got. After all, we had decided not to get married. Allegra and I were numb. Two little automatons said "I will" to the minister and "Sure, sure" to Mother's carefully planned budget and prescriptions. We were to get jobs and save money. In September I would go back to Amherst and Allegra would get a job near school. With luck I'd get my scholarship back, finish in a hurry, get a fellowship to a grad school where Allegra could start work on her BA. We were not to have babies.

Fantastic? We did it and we're still doing it. If not for the draft keeping me in school we would have gone to Europe for a year. Even so, it's not any worse than bingeing around New York or jumping off the Staten Island ferry. For me it's perfect—I have such a strong feeling of righteousness.

But Allegra. She never had those expectations. She never envisioned calm married life overflowing with schoolwork and errands. Oh, most of the time she enjoys it. At least she never complains or tries to change things. But every once in a while she pops. Not after a fight, or before finals, or when we're broke, or connected to any external thing I can figure out. She just pops, maddens, changes, and disappears. And sometimes she doesn't. . . .

So this is one of those nights. She's gone. Bar-bingeing? Flirting with unnecessary drunks. Storing up enough guilt and self-hatred to keep her miserable for months. I try to comb through all my memories to hit upon some pristine principle by which I can understand everything she does. Some detail that will make her life self-evident, obvious. Of course I probably told you the wrong story of her life. This is only one of the stories of Allegra's life. The psycho-sexual development. I could tell you the story of the Bronx: Allegra in her socio-cultural setting. Or a philosophical tale, from hedonism to existentialism to unitarianism.

Put the car keys away, Roger. I'm not going out into the cold night to drag Allegra from someone's bed or beat her bloody. Divorce her, murder her, sit her down and humiliate her. Stop pushing me from the warm chair to the sheetless bed. Let me tell you another story of Allegra's life.

2

—Beeelch.

—Roger. Oh God, Roger, I'm so glad you're here. Whenever I talk for such a long time I feel like I'm alone in an airplane cabin with the pressure leaking out; there's a roar in my ears and I can't tell whether the sounds I hear are coming from within or without. O.K., Roger, would you pull yourself into some sort of a human posture? I'm ready for it. Tell me. Stop smiling that cool disinterested smile. Start judging. What do you think I should do? Speak!

—Well, I think you're a doodie.

—A what?

—A doodie. A juvenile piece of shit.

—Stupid.

—Dummy!

—Roger, you know I'm in trouble. Please be serious. What's a friend for?

—Sissie!

—Roger, don't be a bully. I'm bigger than you.

—Meanie!

—Bossy!

—Ugly!

—Cut it out, Roger. You fuckin' bastard!

—You have bad breath!

—You're ugly and your mother dresses you funny. I'm trying to be serious. You have to tell me what you think. You owe it to me.

—Well, the worst thing you could do to Allegra is make her sit through your version of her life.

—Oh come on, I tried to be fair.

—You're my fraternity brother. I have to tell you. You're a yellow-bellied sapsucker!

—What's that?

—That's what you are!

—All I can say, Roger, is that I hope all your children wear braces.

—And may your mother call you every night.

—And may you be purged from the Socialist club for left-wing deviationism.

—Asshole.

—May you never find anything clever to say again.

—Bllbllbllbllb. May your wife come home and take you off my hands.

—Amen. You know, Roger, you have a really depressing apartment. It hasn't been cleaned in so long it doesn't look dirty anymore. It just looks like everything was meant to be such an ugly color brown. The walls look like the brown-edged pages of old paperbacks. The spring in this chair—

—May you be drafted and sent to Vietnam.

—That's really low. I won't respond to that at all. You're not a bad listener, Roger, but you don't hold up your end of the conversation.

—Allegra says I'm the strong silent type. Did you know that most men who wear glasses have uncommonly small genital organs?

—Did you know that insecurity is the main cause of vulgarity and other forms of low conversation?

—What are you insecure about?

—I think my wife is screwing Kenny Loren.

—Kenny Loren? Why would he want to screw Allegra? He can get any piece in town.

—Do you really believe that?

—Of course I do. You have to get to know Allegra before you want her.

—Do you want to screw her?

—No, but I would love to flaaagellate her. You said I could do it anytime, right?

—Not anytime. Only when we're all drunk and there are hundreds of people around. I don't want it to become an intimate thing. And only if she consents.

—She'll do anything I ask. She respects me.

—Why don't you ask her to stop disappearing?

—Then she'd lose all respect for me. Why don't you ask her? She's already lost all respect for you.

—Why don't you eat it?

—Frig it!

—Suck it!

—Lick it!

—Like it!

—Leave it!

—Lose it!

—I give up. There is one thing I want to say to you, Danny. I'm glad you dropped by tonight. The last time Allegra disappeared you spent all night at Frank Lesser's and I never got to hear the story. Except for the vicious rumors circulating around Hamburger House.

—Moron!

—Minimal brain damage!

—Your syntax is terrible.

—So's yours!

—Roger. I'm not really asking you for advice. I know you're too dumb.

—Recite the amendments to the Constitution.

—Whaaa?

—We'll see who's smarter. Go ahead, D. Yoder, recite.

—I will not. Ask me something else.

—Who are the two ugliest American presidents?

—Lincoln and Taft.

—Wrong!

—What do you mean, wrong?

—Cleveland and Monroe are the ugliest.

—I think Cleveland was kind of cute.

—You're wrong.

—The more hilarious you get, Roger, the more you depress me.

—A few more questions and I'll let you talk for another hour.

—Really?

—What's the most offensive American contraction?

—What?

—Coca-Cola. It should be Coke *of* Cola.

—You're nuts.

—Think about it. Doesn't Coke of Cola sound better? If you say Coca-Cola you'll betray your working-class background.

—I don't have a working-class background.

—The trouble with America today—

—You're making me forget about Allegra.

—Gooo-ness. Sorry to interrupt your brooding. Go right ahead and brood. I'll just sit here and make a list. Lend me your pen.

—What are you listing?

—The troubles with America today.

—What famous authors were doctors, Roger?

—William Carlos Williams. Turgenev. Chekhov. What's the best line of poetry ever written?

—What?

—"My bathrobe is made out of walnuts."

—Who wrote that?

—A girl in my seventh-grade class.

—What famous woman writer died in childbirth?

—There are no famous women writers, Dan.

—You're in good form.

—Shut up and let me write my list.

—Where is Allegra Yoder this very minute?

—Playing third base for the St. Louis Cardinals.

—Maybe I should call the police again. Just for the hell of it. Maybe there was an accident.

—We heard the news four times tonight. If someone loses their cat in Candle City it makes NBC.

—Maybe she got arrested again. Maybe the cops wouldn't let her call me. Or she didn't want to call me.

—I can just see the cops barfing it up at the station. "Hey Sarge, this crazy kid calls up every hour or so to find out if his wife's been arrested. Ha ha, what's he want me to do, make a bed check?"

—Ha ha.

—What did you do last time?

—Which time?

—Any of the other times.

—Oh, lots of different things. None of them worked. Of course I never knew what I was working for. What would you do if you were in my position?

—Move.

—Which way?

—I could never be in your position. I'm going to marry a nineteen-year-old virgin who's never been east of the Mississippi. I'm no fool.

—You're still single.

—There happens to be a shortage of nineteen-year-old virgins in this country.

—I can't sit here all night looking at your cufflink face. Where are the car keys? The bars close in twenty minutes. I've got to find her. I'm too desperate to sit still.

3

Of course I'm stalling! Don't you think I'm aware of that? I'm aware of every pathetic repression, every subconscious shimmer, every guilty, loveless thought that skims over my brain. I'm even aware that my self-awareness is a deception. I'm responsible for everything Allegra does tonight. Before I came down here, Roger, I thought I heard her at the door and was *glad* that it wasn't her. I was enjoying the soul-toughening anxiety. The wrenched bowels.

I'm the bastard of the piece. The bleak truth of the matter is that tonight would have been boring if Allegra came home. We would have talked, eaten dinner, studied, watched a late show, drunk some beers, made love, fallen asleep. We did that yesterday and the day before. Tonight we're pretending we have separate existences. We'll have a lot to blow around tomorrow when she comes home crying onion tears, braced for a blow, biting her lower lip.

Am I moving you, Roger? Am I touching your heart? Don't feel flattered by my confidences. I tell this to everyone, trying to slip out of the stereotypes they clamp on me. I'm not a simple person. I could probably stop Allegra's disappearances if I had one steady response to her. Consistently outraged, abashed, wounded, apathetic. But I am an alternating current. Of course I'm outraged, but I can't hold a grudge longer than the immediate pain. The last time—you wanted to hear about the other times—last time she disappeared I made her see the school psychiatrist. She came home crying, vomited in the toilet, and went to sleep for eighteen hours. When she woke up she said, "Psychiatrists eat shit."

I had to laugh. I should have insisted she continue, but by that time the pure anger and concern had been dissipated; the simplicity of the situation, held together by a single emotion, was shattered into a thousand possibilities and impossibilities. I argued with her, but I was insincere and found myself introducing all sorts of qualifications, arguing her side. She's never willing to debate me, you see, so to be absolutely fair I must bolster her arguments as well as mine. Individual integrity, the right of psychic privacy, psychiatry only helps those who go willingly, new findings in chemistry are disproving Freud every day, what meaning is there in replacing the notion of sin with the notion of neurosis? Oh you can be sure Allegra didn't raise these things. All she said was "I know what's wrong with me. I'm two people, two different people and you have to like both of me." She wouldn't even elaborate the statement, so I did it for her. Allegra the good and Allegra the bad. Allegra the kind pillow of wifely love. Allegra of the hard black eyepits floating on top of a gin-and-tonic with lime juice, spending half my scholarship check on drinks, or worse, letting someone buy them for her. Schizo? Or is it simply the white angel and green devil fighting for possession?

Such sophistry, but I'll latch onto any little explanation she cares to toss at me so I can forget the problem. I have other things on my mind than my wife's disappearances. The split personality argument hums. When I first saw her dragging herself across the floor, red, ugly, lost, Allegra the bad. At our wedding, in white velvet, poised and blushing, Allegra the good. It's much easier to see differences than connections. She stayed in white velvet so long after we were married. I ignored the whole party scene, the entourage of men gathering around her. I pretended only Allegra efficient bed-maker and egg-fryer existed. I tried to shrug off her ever-changing preferences in bed. But it wasn't until she started disappearing that I had to put these things together. I made an honest woman out of her. I expected her to stay honest.

The first time she didn't come home after class I was terrified. Run over? Kidnapped? Did I upset her? Suicide? I prowled the town like a maniac, dashing back every hour to the friend I had posted at the phone. Had she called? Out again, the car overheating, the night coming strongly, my body a network of alarm systems. I found her in the Mainliner, sitting alone, very drunk, at nine p.m. I was annoyed, sarcastic. I sat down and accused: Why didn't you call me? Were you here all this time? I thought you were dead. "I am dead," she said. "Go away." Hard black eyepits, tense fingers, the only thing I recognized were her clothes. I tried to humor her, bought drinks myself, chided her about the money. "I'm not going home"; she said it many times, sometimes arbitrarily, in response to nothing. It was getting later. The bar was filling up with students we knew. They stopped at our booth and I talked to them, but Allegra would not inflect a smile. They moved away. Two hours passed. My skin twitched in annoyance. Let's go home, let's go home, I have an early class tomorrow, I'm tired, I haven't had my dinner, let's go home. She wouldn't respond. The simple fact of the matter is that I'm stronger than you, Allegra, I have you by eleven inches and ninety pounds, let's go. When I grabbed her wrists she began to scream, "Call the police, he's going to kill me, help me, help me, call the police. . . ." She kicked, clinging to the booth. I grabbed her hair, her throat, pulling her into the street, humiliated, horrified. The bartender grinned. Allegra fell asleep in the car on the way home.

The next morning we talked it over. I talked it over, I should say. She made one statement: "I felt different. I felt like it was two years ago and I didn't know you and you had no right to drag me out of the gutter." That sizzled my brain. A question of profound philosophic import: do I have the right to drag Allegra out of the gutter? Am I God, after all? Do I have the right to force her to do good, assuming that I know what's good? Does the marriage license give me the right to save her from self-destruction? If it is self-destruction. If it isn't just blowing off steam. If she is obedient, cheerful, studious most of the time, doesn't she have the right to blast off some of the time? If she has the unalienable right to get drunk alone, don't I have the right to prevent her? License or liberty? Monogamy or monotheism? The drunk binge didn't upset me as much as the thought that men might think she was looking for a pick-up, alone, in a bar. Well? And what if she was? Doesn't she have the right to be unfaithful to me without being physically forced into righteousness, just as I have the right to leave her if I find her unfaithfulness revolting? And a thousand other questions, all raised by me, both sides defended by me, all possible answers defeated by me. The complexity of my mind gets out of hand. Allegra didn't comment on the debate. She just fried up the eggs and bacon, poured the coffee, and shoved a buttered roll into my mouth when my monologue began to give her a headache.

All the questions had been raised and not answered, but I was sure it wouldn't happen again. Two weeks later she didn't come home after French class. Ah ha! This time I would be smarter. I wouldn't wait until she was thoroughly stewed. I dashed over to the Mainliner and asked what her plans were for the evening. Would she like a pizza? A new record album? A punch in the mouth? But as I was pushing her, all the things I said before sounded in my mind. Didn't she really have the right to act against me? "I need to think by myself," she said. "You go home. I'll be along soon." Wouldn't she rather think in a coffee shop, or the library? Wouldn't she rather tell me about it? I had a big paper due the next day, I couldn't sit there all night. "You go home, I'll be right along." Sure, babe. I left. She came home at nine the next morning.

The Ray Charles song, you've heard it:

Believe me friend
It's the living end
When she stays out all night long.
You wrack your brain.
You try in vain
To figure out what you've done wrong.
Well, you know you've got a problem now
And there's nothing that you can do.

I finished my paper that night, too. "The Problem of Succession in the Soviet State." I fell asleep in the chair finally, but sprung awake when I heard her footsteps. The sun glared in my eyes; my head pistoled; I punched her full in the mouth and knocked her out. Her lip bled like a dog. One tooth was pushed so far in I had to pay the dentist ninety dollars to straighten it. For God's sake, if she had only thought up a good excuse. I'd be better off if I were blind like Chaucer's January with a wife who cared enough to lie convincingly.

Ah, that's right, Roger, you only read second-rate American novels published since 1945. January was a blind old man with a young wife. She and her lover would meet up in a tree and make love while January groped around the trunk for his wife. One day a fairy took pity on the old cuckold and gave him back his sight. He looked up and saw the naked couple. His wife, realizing she was caught, said, "I see it worked! The fairy told me if I did this she'd give you back your sight."

I'd be so clever if I wanted to deceive Allegra. I'd pick a used bus ticket off the floor of the Greyhound bus station and tell her I rode all night to St. Louis, repented, and came back. Well, maybe that's not so clever, but it's better than her "I was in the bar. The bar closed. I couldn't walk. Kenny Loren took me up to his apartment and I passed out on the floor and didn't wake up until morning." She cried, I'll say that for her. She bawled through the whole interrogation, nodding yes and no. The tears turned to blood as they ran past her lips. No, he didn't touch me, he didn't rape me, they say he's a fag anyway, my clothes were o.k., you shouldn't have left me there, I was afraid to call you, I forgot the number. She didn't really say those things. When she's quiet it works to her advantage in our fights. She lets me talk myself to death, exhaust myself with possibilities, and finally convince myself of the truth of some version I can live with. We forgave each other and for two months we lived happily ever after.

It happened again. This time I would leave her to her own devices. I wanted to avoid the punching, screaming nausea. This time all the guilt will be hers; I wouldn't participate. She came home at two a.m., drunk, broke, but she came home. I ignored it. I thought of her father and his binges and decided it was hereditary. Occasional drunks are wonderful lovers when they're not drinking. She tried to make it up to me. She never explained, I never asked. It seemed the final solution. As long as she came home at night, I wouldn't ask where she'd been. I really forgot about it until a week later when I was sorting the canceled checks returned by the bank. The one Allegra filled out that night at the Mainliner was endorsed "with love, Kenny Loren." I confronted her. It's a joke, she says, I wouldn't let him buy me

drinks, but I was out of cash so he took my check, it's just a
joke. A great joke. Kenny Loren is a big man; Kenny Loren
owns a bookstore in town and prints the local Socialist sheet
in his cellar. He's forty years old. He probably is a fag. But
I don't really know that, do I?

She disappeared again one day after the check arrived. I
went to the Mainliner. She wasn't there. I went to every bar
in town, twice, describing Allegra. I went to the coffee shops,
the library, the student union, I called the home of every
friend we have. I decided to try Kenny Loren's house. But
he doesn't have a phone and the only way to get to his rooms
is through the bookstore which is closed, and though I bang
and bang on the door there's no response and I can't see any
lights in his rooms though I climb around the back alley and
try to open a window, but they're all sealed and it finally
occurs to me that he may not be home. I try the bars a third
time, this time asking for him, and I'm getting very peculiar
smiles from the bartenders. I think he's out of town; I think I
saw him earlier with his Chicago girl with the glossy black
hair. I saw him in the Mainliner earlier, alone, yes. I think he's
out of town. I'm wondering if he exists at all; an incubus
perhaps. Then the fear sets in. She isn't anywhere. Maybe I
upset her yesterday, maybe she jumped into the river or in
front of a car. Maybe she hopped on someone's motorcycle. I
run home and the phone's ringing as I come in. Allegra. I got
arrested, come get me.

In a little while, darling, I have some studying to do. I
took my time. I felt a pained joy at taking my time combing
my hair, shaving, collecting my checkbook, cigarettes,
glasses, driving very very slowly toward the police station.
It probably took five minutes altogether. Allegra is drunk
but only I can tell it. She's flirting with the policemen and
they're abashed. They let her go without a fine. Drunk and
disorderly, beautiful and free. She told me some story that
time, I guess. Or I told myself some story. Running drunk

down the streets, police ask her where she's going, she wisecracks, they warn her, she gives them the finger, they take her in. Was Kenny Loren in the picture? Was he out of town or running with her or away from her?

Kenny Loren, Kenny Loren. Sounds like a lovesick boy in a ballad. She wouldn't get involved with someone else, I'm almost sure of it. A once fuck, yes; maybe a feel at a party, yes; but again and again, no, I don't think so. She's happy with me. I satisfy her. She has orgasm upon orgasm. She's happy with me. Allegra the good loves me, and even Allegra the bad loves me most of the time. I can't believe she doesn't love me. I've always been loved. I haven't changed. There's no reason not to love me.

But perhaps I'm a cuckold. Cuckold. Cuckadoodle-do. The word is so literary. How nice to typify yourself. A category for Daniel. But I don't believe it! I would know, wouldn't I? I would feel the ashes inside her, I would feel another presence, another smell. I make her happy.

I'm stalling again. I saw that shadow sweep over your sundial face, Roger. The bars are closed now. She'll be home any minute, and if you mention the things I've told you to me tomorrow, I'll deny it all. When Allegra comes home I'll tell her I'll divorce her if she ever disappears again. I'll declaim my lines; I'll act very hard. Maybe she won't know it's an idle threat. Strange things work on her. My most transparent lies convince her more readily than honest attempts to explain myself.

I'll tell her we can have a child if she behaves for a year. A new approach. She wants a child, astounding as that is to me; she wants another plaything, another possession. She may be feeling the mother-urge. I notice she's getting careless about birth-control pills, and we discuss the education of our future progeny. God, if we had a kid I could get a 1Y exemption and wouldn't have to stay in graduate school. I *think* I'd stay in school even if it weren't a good draft dodge, but none of us really knows. Maybe a child would settle her down. Maybe it would be just another thing to neglect.

Tonight, what should I do tonight? I'm really focusing on it, as I'm stalling; I'm trying to think about it. It's just a matter of minutes before she appears. I think I'm using a scientific method to figure her out. Collecting data, sorting and reorganizing, hoping for some flash of revelation. We dehumanize people, punch them out on IBM cards, hoping to rehumanize them at some horizon of insight when the theories will come to life and we'll UNDERSTAND. Then we can act, you see; not an arbitrary action based on *a priori* beliefs, but a beautiful, controlled act, based on sound data.

Did you hear something? I'm working to substantiate a hypothesis: Allegra and I are reversible. Whatever I lack, she has. If we're ever to be saved, it will be a common salvation. We'll enter the kingdom of heaven hand in hand. How can you understand the reverse of yourself? How can you hope to? It's like the teacher of mathematics who can't understand why you don't see the obvious. He never had your problems. He was a math whiz, that's why he's teaching it. He tries to help you but he can't find the source of confusion. He tries to push isosceles triangles in between the baseball cards and rock-and-roll lyrics, but there are no openings. You can't grasp it intuitively and he can't explain it.

I perceive Allegra most clearly in those areas in which she's my opposite, but I can't understand her. Allegra is not a temporal person. She never knows what time it is, what the significance of time is. It's two thirty-five a.m. now. I'll bet she doesn't know that. Why such a fuss about time? She's just not conscious of practical things. She has to look out the window to tell if it's night or day. I'm the opposite. Occupation: clock watcher. "Who do you think you are, Big Ben?" Allegra says. I have a wrist watch, a pocket watch, three alarm clocks in a row on the dresser because we never hear them unless I stagger the rings five minutes apart. Of course I do hear the first ring, but lie there wooing back a dream until at last it dies out and I relax back into sleep and the second one goes off. I wait it out, but the third one goes off before I can arrange the pillow and I'm too irritated to wait through it this time. Then I try to wake Allegra. "It's ten thirty," I say, but it's meaningless to her. So what if it's ten thirty, why should I get up, what's the importance of ten thirty?

It has something to do with laziness. For me time is a moral system. For Allegra the system doesn't exist. Even days and weeks don't exist.

The calendar doesn't punch her into action any more than the clock. Certainly she wants to study, create, learn, but not at this moment when she needs another hour's sleep or she wants to spend the day watching basketball games and thumbing through the *TV Guide.* She can spend a week in her black nightgown staring out the window at the rain, eating cookies. I can't fathom that in her. I have to work, or actively enjoy myself. I can't just lie back and let the world flow past for hours and days. If I want to waste time I want to see a movie, drive in the country . . . We should be one person, you see. One person who is both timely and timeless, lazy and zealous, gay and depressed. If she's out there destroying herself, I'm in here suffering for her. When I fall into my fits of tension, she's calm for me. We don't miss anything that way; we can have discordant experiences without sacrificing our individual integrity.

Oh, God, do you hear me? Am I just babbling? Am I neatly stacking data cards on the table, waiting for the janitor to come and burn the trash? Allegra—can I find her in this web of information? Is she there at all? I am suffering very hard for her. It's two forty. I am tearing at my flesh and sitting in uncomfortable positions so I can wear her ashes on my brow. We'll be running out of beer soon, Roger, running out of throat-grease and temple-coolers. If I can drink

myself stupid before the beer runs out I won't go back to my
apartment tonight. When Allegra wanders in, the house will
be empty. Then she'll have a flash of fear. She'll run down to
see you, Roger, and you can tell her I'm out cold in the
bathtub and she's a dirty bitch for doing this to me. You'll
condemn her, won't you, Roger? But first you have to
understand me, to see exactly what part I play in this game,
how cowardly and ineffectual and unloving I am.

I wish something disastrous would happen to me before
she comes home. I could throw myself against the window
and scar my face. I could crack my skull in the bathtub. I
could hold my breath until I died. Then she'd be sorry. I
could twist my arm as hard as I can, snap my wrist, and dan-
gle that in front of her astonished face.

Maybe I don't satisfy her. She's greedy; she wants many
many objects, an abundance of gestures, kisses from over-
kissed lips, touches until the skin aches. She never desires a
single thing. I can't see her having one lover. Many lovers,
thousands of lovers, perhaps. Sometimes she tears through
stamp-redemption catalogues, counting our books over and
over, calculating future books, desiring plastic, aluminum,
Teflon, chrome-coated, electrically powered, remote-con-
trolled everything. The greed comes in a fit and is exhausted,
but never sated. She grows contemptuous of the coveted
kitchen conveniences. Her desires will subside for a time, and
then reignite in visions of suede suits and coats, velvet slippers, bright, long bathrobes, diamond bracelets, two, three,
twelve dangling on her wrist, a delicate profusion; dozens of
the softest nylon stockings of blue, beige, black sparkling
gauze. Even in gardening she demands excess: she never thins
the flower beds enough. She wants fresh flowers to fill every
vase, glass, teapot, aspirin bottle in the house, thick bright
bouquets of fragrant flowers, swooningly sweet, in all sea-
sons, lilacs and lilies and irises and plum blossoms. When she's
shopping, even in the supermarket, her fingers quarrel with

the temptation to touch every item, to pile up a mountain of groceries, to fall on the bed caressing the tin cans and boxes.

She is sure each new possession will bring her happiness. I hate myself when I remind her she is always disillusioned. Often before we get home with the bright curtain material, long before it's been sewn into café curtains swinging from adorable brass loops, she'll regain her intelligence and realize they won't change her life, and plunge into depression. She'll be void of desire for weeks, and then another advertisement will flare up some need and she'll decide our life would be perfect if we had the security of a well-stocked liquor cabinet, an assortment of liqueurs, whiskeys, and wine, heavy on the gin.

I tend to savor each individual purchase we make, drawing unreasonable amounts of happiness from it so I can justify the expenditure months after it's been made. I fling my trenchcoat over my shoulders, still admiring and savoring it. I watch Allegra slip on those two-ninety-five flimsy gold earrings. . . . That's a beautiful sight, I tell you, watching her stick the cold metal rods through the blood-rimmed holes in her ears.

She tries to make me participate in mental buying orgies, hoping to motivate me, I guess, to make enough money to keep her in nylons someday. We read of a contest in which the winner and his family were to be given ten minutes in Groggin's department store to snatch whatever they please. All they could carry, load in carts, and roll behind the finish line—but only ten minutes. We didn't enter the contest because we didn't eat that brand of cereal, but we talked and talked about what we would do if we won. I would stake the store out in advance, I decided, and dash for the diamonds. Allegra. What would you take, Allegra? Lingerie, she said at first, dozens and dozens of nightgowns to bewitch you with. Or dresses, shoes, handbags, or perhaps the kitchen department with their large ceramic bowls and candlestick holders in star shapes, sedate linen tablecloths, sheets of every possible color. Whatever Allegra wants she wants in all the possible colors. She can never choose a color, so I gave her this rule: when in doubt, choose blue. She follows the rule. When in doubt, Allegra, come home.

Emergencies like this are exhilarating, you must admit. I refuse to rise to the circumstances. My adrenal glands don't goad me on to heroic action. But I'm a fan of spectacular, eccentric happenings. If I have to do research in old newspapers, it takes me hours and hours because I'm distracted by the murder stories, the visit of the Queen of New Zealand, and miss the passage of the farm bill I'm looking for. I like issues of minimal importance. My wife disappears occasionally. That sets me apart from the happily married crowd. Last winter, surplus Chicago snow was loaded into boxcars and shipped south. I can deal with a story like that. Much easier than trying to comprehend that our planes have flown twenty thousand bombing missions over North Vietnam since February.

I understand the type of people who loot stores better than the boys who burn draft cards. I always curdle when I pass lovely appliance displays covered with artificial snow. I'm waiting for the moment when I can smash a flimsy glass and dash home with a color television. What would you do if the lights went out, Roger? Who would you murder if the state crumbled? Where will you be when the bombs drop? Don't mock me—these are ultimate questions. Whose panties would you dive for in a panty raid?

At this rate I'll be goo-goo by the time I reach the White House. That's still part of the master plan, you know, mother's manual for expectant presidents. "You have a calling for politics," my mother says, "the way other men have a calling for the ministry." All the time I was reading *The New York Times* she never realized I was reading between the issues.

When my mother told Allegra I was going to be president, Allegra giggled. My mother twitched her nose twice and explained how my brilliant dissertation-to-be on American political structure would astound the nation with *the* answer, reconciling capitalism and communism, Freud and Marx, God and the antihero. I would become the idol of youth. While I waited to pass thirty-five I'd teach courses at Harvard and serve on presidential advisory committees, visit the Soviet Union, run for the Senate on a daring reform program, emerge victorious, grinning, destined for the White House. Allegra laughed like boiling water. She still claims she thought it was a joke. Note the little variations from the obvious in Mother's plans. No law school in the picture—law dulls the mind. No war record—I might get killed. No elaborate connections, power groups, popular policies—I am to be president by sheer weight of my intellectual and personal virtues. You understand this, Roger; your parents also raised you to be president.

I've shrunk over the years. Mother's dreams were based on some reality. I glittered when I was young. I was decisive, active, happy. Oh, the burden of a happy childhood. I've always envied bastards, orphans, children of divorce. How free they must be! My parents gave me a happy childhood and a bearable adolescence. Now they want my life in return.

I keep Allegra around to stub my toe on when I'm trying to climb into my parents' dreams. She's a reminder of my despicable . . . What shall I do? Shall I find a shotgun and blast her out of Kenny Loren's bed?

I'm such a champion at raising uncomfortable questions. And leaving them unanswered.

It's three o'clock. She won't come home now. I'm not angry. I'm puzzled. That curly-haired boy sitting in a stream of sunlight on the kitchen floor learning to tie his shoes: how did he turn into a paralyzed man who can't find the answer that *must* be self-evident in all this information?

4

—I'm finished with my list. Do you want to hear it?

—What list?

—The troubles with America today. There are two columns: not enough and too much. The trouble with America today is that there's not enough:

college students with working-class backgrounds
strong, manly frontier-type men
nineteen-year-old virgins
hate and rebellion radiating from the lower classes
depravity and licentiousness.

The trouble with America today is that there's too much:

Coke of Cola
presidential power
bombing
money
miracles
statistical studies
sagging enemy morale.

—That's wonderful, Roger. I must say I'm glad Allegra disappeared tonight just so I could have the opportunity to witness the creation of such a wonderful list.

—You really like it?

—Sagging enemy morale was o.k. You ought to work in that phrase they used on the news tonight: "We are no longer losing the war."

—Do you think we can blame the war for our degeneracy? I trust you, Dan; if you say yes, I'll believe you. Alice Little says I'm a *de*generate because I poured beer down her blouse.

—That was a great party. I think we can blame the war for that party. How many of us overgrown students would even be in this town if not for the war? Allegra and I were going to spend the year in Europe. But who do you blame the war on? I asked the kids at the teach-in that question and they asked it right back to me. It couldn't be Johnson, they said, because Kennedy started it. It couldn't be America, because France started it. The question came up when they were trying to pick a spot to burn their draft cards. They're going to do it in front of the post office, because that's the only Federal building in town.

—Well, I think we can certainly blame the post office for the war, and for Alice Little's party too!

—School must really be dulling our minds, Roger. I used to be brilliant. And you occasionally said things that made sense.

—I'm about to say something that makes sense. Are you ready for this?

—Yeah.

—I want you to go upstairs and bring down some blankets and your pillow. I want you to go to sleep. I'm really tired. If I don't get a couple of hours' sleep tonight, my crash-cool program will be ruined.

—Ah, I knew something was going on. I saw that sunlamp rigged up above the toilet. I saw that body-building magazine.

—The truth is, Dan, I've been noticing my popularity is not what it used to be. I'm five pounds heavier. I have that haggard look from sleeping crazy hours. I'm nearing a personal crisis. So I have reinstituted my old three-point program: sunlamp, exercise, and five consecutive hours of sleep a night. And here it is my second day and you're keeping me up all night.

—I can't go upstairs. I'll kill myself if I see that empty apartment.

—Dan! I want you to . . . I had this dream last night. I'm walking down a skid row street and I turn down an alley and this hoodlum jumps on me, kicks me in the balls, in the stomach, beats me up. I lie there awhile, then get up and the dream starts again. I'm walking down the same filthy street and I turn down the same alley and a fat Negro man with a cigar jumps me, beats me up, and sticks his cigar in my stomach. Again—I'm walking down the alley and two boys, no bigger than twelve, jump me and start punching into me. They leave me lying down next to a garbage pail. I lie there thinking it over and I have a revelation. I pull myself behind the pail and wait. A nice-looking, clean-cut college kid comes walking down the alley and I jump out and start beating the hell out of him.

—Roger, that's a fine dream! I didn't know you had dreams.

—Get upstairs and get those blankets!

—Look, I can't . . .

—Dan, that nice-looking, clean-cut college kid in my dream looked a lot like you. Come on, I'll walk upstairs with you.

—What do you mean, you'll walk me? I'm not that cowardly. I mean, I may not want to fight in Vietnam, but that doesn't mean I'm afraid of all risks. I mean it *is* my own apartment. Do you think she might be up there?

—No.

—Then what's the use? To have concrete proof my wife is missing? The place is such a mess. We were going to clean it up this afternoon—maybe that's why she disappeared. She's so funny about those things. Did I ever tell you about the great food struggles we had right after we were married?

—Get the blankets, Dan.

—No, wait a minute. This is really a great story.

—You're stalling.

—Look, you know when I want to tell a story I just have to tell it. You can't put me off. You could throw me out the window and I'd scream the story as I fell.

—Tell me on the way up there.

—Let me tell it first! I can't walk well when I'm talking. Come on, Roger, you'll love it, you don't know anything about that part of our lives. I was working in an ice-cream factory in New York and Allegra was working—

—I'm so tired my face is sagging.

—Hang in there, Roger. You'll get a second wind. Where was I? Allegra was working in a five-and-ten store. I was aware when I married her that she wouldn't be an ideal domestic servant, but I expected her to try. I tossed her in the kitchen with a fair assortment of electrical equipment and said, Be a wife. Pour the coffee, clean the house, fulfill the whole complex of notions I got from my mother. I won't say Allegra revolted. She never acknowledged my expectations. If she was hungry she opened a can of salmon and gave the juice to the cat. She saw no reason why I couldn't do the same. And I *had* been doing the same for two years of college, but now . . . I had a wife, damn it. She wouldn't discuss the situation. When she came home from work she drank beer and looked in the mirror with her face squashed over her fist. I walked around the house kicking at piles of underwear, lecturing on domestic science. One day I had a regular tantrum. A man yearns for pot roast! I shoved a pressure cooker and a five-pound chuck roast at her and said, Cook it or I'll kick your head in. She was amused, obedient. She blew the top off the pressure cooker and served me half-raw pot roast dressed with plaster chips. You just can't push her around. We ate in bar-and-grills. Then she moved, in her own way. One day she bought a seven-ninety-five illustrated cookbook and sat all weekend looking at the pictures. Then —zap—I was eating strange foods with wine sauces, home-made salad dressings, pancakes for breakfast. And she seemed to get a kick out of making these things. She didn't sulk. She charged around tinkling her measuring spoons, talking to her garlic press.

—Finished?

—Just about the same thing happened with housekeeping, although that came a few months later.

—The trouble with you two is you eat too good. If you ate canned franks and beans you'd be as manly as I am. Hate-food. There's nothing like franks and beans from the can to make you hate all the people eating better than you. All people earning over ten thousand a year should be shot.

—Including your parents?

—Especially my parents! Where do they get off, having all that money while I'm eating canned franks and beans? You know, Dan, that was a real interesting story about you and Allegra and all. Now let's go up to your apartment—

—How many cans of franks and beans do you have in the house?

—Maybe seven.

—Let's open them all up and stand by the window. When Allegra comes home tonight we'll throw them on her head.

—Take it easy.

—I wish I were drunker.

—There's only a few more beers.

—There's some bourbon up in my apartment.

—I don't believe you.

—There is! Not too much, maybe four shots. Stop shak-ing your head. It's left over from a bottle Allegra's father gave us.

—I don't believe it would have lasted this long.

—I've got it hidden, right up on top of the closet where we throw things when we're cleaning up the house. Come on up and I'll show you if you don't believe me.

—You're not the type to hoard bourbon.

—Come up with me. We can get those blankets. Who knows, Allegra might be there.

—All right, you lying creep. Just let me put on my shoes.

—Notice how this staircase smells like every other staircase in the world. Dark, creaky, a slight smell of franks and beans. Maybe I'll just sit on the stairs all night with a hammer in my hands and when she comes home I'll smash her brains in.

—The door's locked. Why's the door locked?

—Oh, I locked it in case Allegra came home when I was sleeping in your house; she'd have to come downstairs for the key and I'd—

—Where's the key?

—Downstairs.

—For God's sake—

—It's o.k., I can open it with a butter knife. You run downstairs and get me a butter knife. I'll kick the door in the meantime.

—Hold on a minute! You haven't got your shoes on. Just wait here—

—Hurry up, Roger, hurry. Alone in front of a locked door in a forty-watt smelly hallway. I'll give you thirty seconds to come home, Allegra. This is the perfect moment. No one will see how tenderly I welcome you back. Where's the butter knife? God damn it, Roger, I wanted to open the door with a butter knife. What's the challenge of putting a key in the hole—let me do it!

—Where's the bourbon?

—On top of the closet. You get it while I check the bedroom.

—There's no bourbon up here. Just stockings and news-papers and stuff . . . well look at this. My raspberry bath-robe. What's my raspberry bathrobe doing in this closet?

—That's Allegra's.

—She gave it to me. I admired it so much she gave it to me to drape around girls after I made love to them.

—Allegra's not here. Unless she's hiding.

—How did it get back here?

—You threw it out the window one night, Roger, remem-ber? You said every time you looked at it you remembered how you never got a chance to drape it around a girl.

—Where's the bourbon?

—Oh, isn't it there? I guess we must have finished it.

—Yeah, like last January.

—There's some beer in the refrigerator. Give me a hand, there's some hamburger and cheese and bacon . . . do you have any mayonnaise? O.k., we'll leave that. But take the coffee and cherry jam—that's my favorite jam.

—What the hell are you doing?

—I'm going to strip this apartment bare and leave the door wide open.

—Just get a blanket, Danny. You don't need this stuff.

—Milk, applesauce, leftover *daube de boeuf*. Hey, we had this stuff last night, Roger, and it was great. Why don't I heat some up? You put the stuff back in the refrigerator and . . . you look so funny, Roger, standing there with an armful of cold groceries. Put that stuff back, will you? Will you close the refrigerator door, Roger? What the hell's the matter with you? Will you sit down? Come on, open up some beers and sit down.

—Danny, I'm getting tired of being your best friend. Why don't we switch roles—you be my best friend.

—O.k. Let me get this baby into the oven. Open the beers; that's it, lie down on the couch, Roger. Green and yellow floral chintz; it's really much more comfortable up here than at your house. That's it, relax, Roger. Take your shoes off before you put your feet on the couch, you lummox.

—Goodnight. When you feel sorry for me, Dan, you can put a cover over me.

—Roger? Roger, I know you think I'm disgusting. But to show you what a true friend I really am I'm going to let you fall asleep. I'll just shut up, that's all. I won't bother telling you about the last time I was this depressed. I know you'll want to hear this one, Roger. It was the first time a girl told me she loved me. Her name was Regina. I went with her all through high school. She had a long dark ponytail, long skinny legs, a high-school queen, a teenage dream. But she was so straight. I told her I loved her. I must have told her a million times, every time I was trying to sneak my hand into her tight white bra. And she would tense up and say, Now listen. That's all. I'd stop and listen but she never said anything else. She got me so worked up I couldn't wait to dash home and jerk off. Then a couple of weeks before graduation we were necking in my parents' basement; I was trying to wiggle a finger under the tight bra strap saying, Regina, I love you, I love you so much, Regina, and she said, I love you, Danny. I stopped dead. My hand numbed. I realized I didn't love her at all, that I was a fiendish manipulator trying to get something off her just like she always thought. I was appalled that I had been telling a girl for three years that I loved her when I actually didn't. So I asked her to marry me. That's my normal reaction when I realize I'm in a bad situation: plunge in deeper. We became secretly engaged and she let me feel her breasts, but not look at them. Then we both went off to college. She broke up with me after she got my first letter which said something like, One of the first things I've learned in college, Regina, is that when people are in love they give themselves to each other without hesitation or inhibition. And today that girl is unhappily married to a high-school math teacher who has a thing for little boys. Roger? That was an interesting story, wasn't it, Roger? Roger!

5

When was the time for all good men? Allegra once flipped out in the supermarket trying to choose a detergent. Twenty-three brands of detergent at last count. Altogether too many brands of detergent. White granules in green boxes, blue tablets in cellophane sacks, cold-water, hot-water, hard-water, wet-water soaps, sudsy and sudsless, perfumed and pre-softened, bleached and safe for clothing you wouldn't dare bleach, extra tough, extra gentle, extra special, thirteen cents off, free diaphragm enclosed, big size, bigger size, bigger-than-you-can-believe size for only half the price, Swish, Swallow, Gulp, Swim, Blow, Pow, Punch, Sock, K.O., Pitch, Puke, M'Lady's Little Helper. Allegra began to tremble. Did she want a bright, light, flighty wash, or a tense, tight, hysterically sanitary wash? If you were a detergent, which brand would you be? She rubbed her forehead with a can of frozen orange juice. I, ever in control, studied all the labels, divided the prices by the ounces by the cupfuls per wash load and chose the brand my mother uses. You can't let these things get the best of you.

Even sensitive idealists have to learn to live in the world.

It's a matter of methodology, mechanics. Mind reading is one of my mechanisms. One day the university paid me four dollars an hour to guess cards and I guessed fifty percent more accurately than pure chance could explain. Congratulations, you have extra-sensory perception. Oh, was I excited! What should I do with it? Conquer the world? Predict elections? Just forget it, they said, a lot of people have it. Forget it? One of the most exciting moments of my life . . . forget it?

I've been working hard on mind reading, using Allegra as my prime subject. It's nice to know what's happening in your wife's head. It came very easily at first. I stepped on all her sentences. "Would you—" "Pour the coffee? Sure." "Let's—" "No, four late shows a week are quite enough." "Please—" "We'll go to sleep as soon as I finish reading this chapter." But all this is not too significant. Most married couples achieve some degree of psychic communication. She pretended to be completely amazed, humoring me. I tried harder. I left the bedroom before she got dressed in the morning and wrote down what I thought she'd wear. About eighty-percent accurate. I predicted her test marks. Ninety-five-percent accurate at an .01 level of confidence. I guessed what days and times her mother would call. Perfectly accurate.

So on to bigger things. Could I predict when she was going to disappear? If you know the future, you can alter it—isn't that the premise of all those science-fiction movies? Every day I wait for her in front of the Modern Language Center. Will she or won't she appear? I always guessed she would. She did. Except when she didn't. Like today. I'm apparently unable to predict her disappearances, but that doesn't lessen my faith in mind reading. Wish interferes with guess, you see. I want her to trot down the steps, waving her French book; I can't guess otherwise.

Tonight . . . can you call four a.m. tonight, or is it last night? Tonight I'm going to call her into conversation. I just want her voice, not her image. Her sunflower face is distracting. Why penetrate such an appealing surface? But I want to hear her voice, out of the range of my glares and fists.

Allegra? Leggie? Legs? Allegra!
[There's no hope for a mind that's lost its message and meandered into meadows where thoughts flip through faster than a fall frolic and the meanings are not clear.]
Not clear. Are you there?
[The message has meandered into meadows of the coldest November drafty-bit.]
Oh claptrap.
[Same to you, Danny-boy.]
Your voice sounds like an echo of my own. Where are you?
[She took a plane to Paris, France, to do a dance in her underpants.]
What's the matter with you?
[When I have a daughter I'm going to tell her! It's inexcusable to repeat the same mistake for two generations. I'll tell her so early she won't have a chance to get messed up. If I were my daughter I wouldn't be messed up. She'll be perfectly beautiful, or unbearably ugly, not middling like me.]
You're very beautiful, Allegra.
[Occasionally, in the right dress, right mood, right light, I'm irresistible. But when my hair curls up, or my skin is murky from the heat or red from the cold, when I slouch around in dungarees . . . The construction men didn't whistle at me today. The turkeys didn't peep out of the straw. They didn't look up from the hole they were digging. Humiliated on the way to school.]
I love you.
[Since when were you a great judge of beauty? You couldn't tell a goldfinch from a turkey. It's almost an insult to be called beautiful by you. It's the strangers that have to

look, the ones that don't know I'm also very bright and have a lovely personality.]

You're not supposed to care about strangers.

[I know, marriage was supposed to end all that. My substitute for the one big bang. When I was twelve I wanted one long big satisfying exhausting exhilarating boom that would free me of the sex thing for the rest of my life. So I had that one big long and about three days later . . . So marriage, getting it without plotting, teasing, flirting, that was the substitute. Don't let anyone tell you, daughter, that marriage ends all that. It's not enough that Daniel says wow, growl, what a dress, kiss, grab, smack, a knock-out you are. Not nearly enough.]

Tell me what to do.

[Let's have all boys, sons. Not that guys have it any easier. I feel sorry for them. All the blond-haired guys tensed up inside their beige dungarees when I passed tonight. It's painful for them, trying to get inside some professional virgin, all the time wondering if they're latents or something. I'd like to sit on the curb and offer my mouth to all.]

Tell me what to do.

[Don't read my mind. Read my Rh factor or something. Can you read it? Negative, like the rest of me.]

Tell me what to do.

[You don't pat my ass enough. You're too absorbed in your stinking books to pat my ass. You don't pull my hair. You never call me Blondie.]

Blondie?

[I always wanted to be called Blondie.]

Your hair is red.

[What did you always want to be called?]

Rock.

[No kidding? Once I was standing near a bar waiting for a bus and a man weaved over to me and said, Come on, Blondie, I'll buy you a drink. Once when I was twelve years

old the ice-cream man said, I'll give you forty dollars if you
go in the bushes with me, Blondie. I ran all the way home.]
I'll kill him. I'll kill both of them.
[They're already dead. The drunk was killed by a car.
The ice-cream man stepped on a land mine forty miles north
of Saigon. I still dream about him. His name was Tony.]
What do you dream about?
[Read my dreams if you're so smart.]
I can't read minds in my sleep.
[I dream about sex. That's what you wanted to hear, right?
I dream about sexual perversions, beating, whipping, sucking
in forty-three positions, dressed in black spangles, spankings,
beads, long black stockings, slave auctions, bestiality . . .]
You're lying!
[You're the mind reader. I never argue with my mind
reader. What do you think I dream about?]
Parties.
[One-hundred-percent accurate.]
Tell me.
[You're right. I dream about parties. If we were going to
a party tonight I wouldn't have disappeared. I love parties.
Party party. When I was a little girl I had the prettiest party
dress—blue lacy layers on layers and it swung way out when
I turned and it had white pearls sewn on the lace, little pearl
buttons down the front, puffy sleeves and a matching blue
slip, matching blue panties and matching blue socks with my
name embroidered on them. I just couldn't wait until I was
invited to a party. Then the day came and my father drove
me and I stood in the doorway while the boy's mother said
what a pretty pretty dress you have. Then I looked at the
other girls. They were wearing sleek little shifts with stockings and high heels and looked five years older than the boys.
It was too late for my party dress.]
I've heard that story a dozen times.
[But it never loses its charm, right? I didn't wear stock-

ings, I wore undershirts. My hair was in little fat curls. I looked like a baby!]

Don't cry.

[Ten years old and I looked like a baby! My legs were too skinny for nylons. The stores didn't have stockings that small, or bras that small. It was awful!]

Party party.

[Party party. It's different now, isn't it?]

Very different.

[Now they look at me when I come into the room and they don't think I look like a baby.]

A beautiful baby.

[I'm short.]

Short enough.

[You're tall.]

Incredibly.

[And yet we're compatible. Isn't that something? Kenny Loren is short.]

Why did you say that?

[It's true, isn't it? Kenny Loren is quite short for his age.]

He's forty.

[And quite short.]

Are you sleeping with Kenny Loren?

[Read my mind.]

I can't. I just read my wishes.

[Let's put it this way. If I were having an affair, you can bet your boots it would be with Kenny Loren. If. I were. But of course I'm not. Probably. Isn't he a fag?]

How should I know? Why Kenny Loren?

[He's short.]

You said you always planned to marry someone tall.

[True. But indiscretions with short men. So you can beat them up easily when you find out. I have your interests at heart, you see.]

Kenny Loren?

[Stud. Or fag. Or both. Probably both. Isn't that interesting? I always planned to have affairs with interesting men.]
Allegra!

[Party party. You can't boss me around like that. What makes you think I'll take it? No more parties, you say, no more parties. Then I have to find other excitements.]

Just until the end of the term. We both have to get our work done. Just until—

[Every Saturday night there's a party. But I never get to go anymore. I love parties. I have a new knit black mini-dress that fits like a slip and makes my legs look longer than a five-foot person's could ever be. I want to wear my new dress. I want all the boys to flip out and under and pet me with their eyes and ask me to dance every dance so they can see my legs move to the fast music and feel my body in the slow ones. Then when you get drunk and get into one of your *in*tellectual conversations, they walk me to the kitchen to get another drink and try to kiss me, or casually feel my bust and pat my ass and tell me I'm the best-looking chick in town and isn't it a shame I'm a very faithful wife? Yes, yes, Allegra, it's really a pity. They drop something and pick it up and run their hands up my stockings all the way to my waist, and I'm very brusque and say cut it out, then scream cut it out, but you don't hear me, so brother Roger, drunk and ever looking for a fight, will run into the kitchen and bop them on the head. Then there's a fight—over me—a fistfight. Poor Roger gets beaten up because he can't fight when he's drunk. You finally show up to defend him and it turns into a dazzling free-for-all and we all dig it until we hear the cop sirens. Then it's quick, quick, get your coats, quiet, smiling, the cops are gentlemen—please turn the phonograph down—and then the best part. For days, weeks after, you tell all our friends who weren't at the party how someone tried to grab me and Roger defended me and how exciting. And the boys sit there thinking yes, I understand why someone would grab her; and the girls think yes, I understand why they would defend her. You tell the story much more exciting than it really was. Roger sits there nodding, flexing his biceps.]

Party party.

[You love them too, I know it. It gives you a stiff erection every time you see some other guy looking me over lasciviously.]

That's not true!

[What's the word ... voyeurism?]

You look great on those days. That's what arouses me.

[Oh, you get an erection at the party, all right, but then you expend all that vigor in drinking, fighting—by the time we get home you can't perform at all. Fourteen guys have done your foreplay, but you haven't the energy to—]

Shut up!

[On other nights you're fine. Monday, Thursday, anytime after I've washed the floors or studied until my eyes ache, then you're all hot. But Saturday nights—]

Christmas, Humphrey Bogart, Humpty Dumpty, money, Hegel!

[Party party.]

I told you, anytime you felt like disappearing we'd find a party to go to. If you told me in advance—

[We would have discussed it. And discussed it. Why exactly was I feeling like going to a party? Why on this very night before the day you had something phenomenally important to do?]

Those parties aren't for married people. Guys go there to make girls. Girls hope for a ride home to the happily ever after. We don't belong there.

[So that's why I didn't tell you in advance. Just disappeared. Poof! Gone! To where? Destination unknown. Some cold November meadow where thoughts flip through faster than a fall frolic.]

What's that music I hear?

[It's the Muzak. They play it at all the best mental hospitals to keep your nerves calm. I find myself humming songs I hate, hating myself for humming songs I hate to hum.]

Don't you want to come home now? There are no sheets on the bed. You have to make the bed. I won't be angry if you come home now. You curl into a curlicue on the bed and I'll curve around you and stroke your hair and call you Blondie. And when you scream at dawn I'll throw my arms around you before I wake you up so you won't be frightened.

[And if I'm lucky I won't remember what I dreamt about.]

What do you dream about?

[Woman sinning and bitchery.]

Come home.

[I'm locked in.]

Tell me where you are. I'll come for you. I won't be angry.

[I'm on a Boeing DC-7 flying over Laramie, Wyoming. The sky is black. The other passengers are sleeping, dozing, except for a small redhead in a black knit mini-dress who's leaning over the captain's shoulder while he explains what all those pretty dials mean. The redhead's husband is engrossed in a discussion about the plane's safety features with the first mate and doesn't notice the captain's hand skidding up his wife's nylons.]

I think reading your mind bores me.

[_____]

Allegra? I didn't marry you for your lovely personality. You don't have a lovely personality and you're not all that bright. Come home and toss on the sheets. Allegra?

[I'm hurt.]

Where are you?

[I'm twelve years old and I've just been screwed and I'm thinking it all over. Trying to fit things in. I'm giggling. I found out I'd never been a virgin. What a sign! What if I had waited and waited until I was twenty, putting off my fiancé until the wedding night. . . . It really struck me funny. The lesson seemed so obvious. I didn't go to parties then—I went on heavy dates because screwing was the royal entertainment. But now. If I'm to be faithful to you I have to have lots of parties, lots of strangers crawling their hands around me. . . .]

That's enough. Goodbye.

[I'm not the type of current you can just turn off. The media is me, internalized, woven through all your tiny brain waves.]

Boy, this beer is good. I'm kind of glad Roger fell asleep; that leaves two more for me. When I finish this beer I'll have another. Another.

[Ah, but that moment of crystal clarity as the image shrinks. That last flash of light before the final dissolve.]

Maybe I'll just spread the blanket over the mattress. . . . Where are you?

[Not very far away. Not that you've tried hard to find me. You stretch out your arms and if I don't come, you clutch your sides and suffer.]

Do you want a divorce?

[My God, Daniel, what would mother say? If Adlai Stevenson hadn't been divorced he might have been president. You're going to risk all that just to get rid of a small section of brain cells that speaks out against the rest?]

I'm turning my mind off. You don't exist.

[Goodnight, sweet child. Goodnight, you brilliant beautiful boy whispering to the gritty mattress that someday, someday, you're going to be very very happy and it's just a matter of surviving and enduring until that someday comes, because it's bound to come, it has to come, you're all grown up now, two thousand miles from mommy and daddy, with a car of your own, a car of your own, a car—]

Cut it!

[A car. C-A-R. Of your own. Car. Automobile. Ford.
Buick. Volkswagen . . .]
It's not true. What you're going to say is simply not true.
[I was in the Mainliner until two a.m. tonight. Two a.m.
I gave you every chance to come and get me. Where the hell
were you? You didn't come because you're afraid to get in
the c-a-r.]
You want me dead!
[If you're going to get hysterical I'll just turn off the
light and doze off. I'm quite drunk myself, remember. I could
fall asleep before you could say: The reason I didn't look for
you tonight, Allegra, is that I was afraid to get in the car
and kill—]
Click. _____

There are times of course when I'm not in the mood to read
my wife's mind. Times I simply don't care to. Wake up,
Roger; wake up, you fuck! Go wash your face. I'm drinking
your share of the beer, Roger.

[Click. You haven't got the only switch, you know. My
mind is in a very public mood. It demands reading. Read!
Listen, I'll read my thoughts aloud. Thoughts you haven't
the nerve to think yourself. Car. C-A-R! You were afraid to
get into the car tonight. You're always afraid to drive when
you're upset, but that doesn't mean you'll ever let me drive.
You're a coward. Oh, you're pretty brave with your fists,
and mouth off a lot to authority figures, but in the car you're
a coward.]
That's ridiculous. I'm simply a sensible driver. It's a sign
of maturity that I don't drive—
[I think it's a sign of senility.]
Unless I feel up to it emotionally.
[Which you didn't tonight.]
I don't know. I didn't think about it. I wanted you to

come home of your own volition. I didn't want to drag you out of a bar—

[Into the car. I know exactly what went through your mind. You could have walked over to the Mainliner, but after that full confession of fear last time—]

This is unnecessary. I won't accept your guilt. You can't project it on me.

[You're doing the reading, remember? I'm not even there. Last time I disappeared you crashed the car into a ditch.]

It was just an accident. You're no one to talk about—

[A very peculiar accident, the way you told it. You were driving along wondering what would happen if you went into a ditch and the thought frightened you so you said hell, there's nothing to be afraid of, and drove the car into the ditch to prove it. Driving along the ditch like a damn cowboy. But it didn't quite work out that way. You flattened four tires, dented the bumper, and did who knows what internal damage. . . .]

I'm immune to your accusations. You choose not to come home. It's all your fault, no matter what you say about cars and parties, no matter how inadequate I am.

[That was eloquent. Think what Mother would say if you had another accident. Insurance rates so high, and this car has to last until you get your Ph.D., which is at least a decade away. Wouldn't Mother be miffed!]

You're a fool to make fun of that. I'm a very safe driver. I've never had one moving violation.

[When I ride next to you, listening to your incessant remarks about all the crazy drivers on the road and how poorly banked the highway is and why they don't have a stop sign at this very dangerous corner—it makes me sick.]

You never say anything. You always go to sleep in the car. You have no idea how I drive.

[I have memories of other drives, other drivers. When I was thirteen I rode in chicken races.]

I heard that story. Why don't you swing your legs off that bed? If you want to be unfaithful to me, do it in the daytime. I don't care all that much.

[Are you giving me permission?]

Are you sleeping with Kenny Loren?

[Oh for Christ's sake, you wouldn't be happy no matter what I answered.]

Yes I would. I'd be very happy if you said no. A definitive no.

[No. Certainly not! What an outrageous suggestion!]

Then where are you? I called the cops; you're not in jail or the morgue. Kenny Loren is the only one I can think of without a phone.

[He hates phones. He firmly believes that news can wait till morning.]

You barely know him.

[He pities me. He thinks you're a rotten husband to be afraid to get in your car and take me home. He thinks I'm mentally disturbed, messed up, misunderstood.]

Perceptive.

[Now's the time to say the right thing.]

I'm going to use the bathroom now. I'm glad I'm home instead of at Roger's. His bathroom is cold and bare and dirty. Ours has a hairy bathmat to warm my toes. Oil-soft lotions in powder sprays amid the limp stockings crossing their legs over the shower rack. Woody pine, lemon-lime, floral cream, sinful dream. Thick blue towels to sooth a dripping face. Deep green toilet paper. The bank clock blinking time and temperature through the bathroom window. Four forty-eight. Eighteen degrees. It's time to come home now. You also hate strange bathrooms. Come home to me, the ultimate audience.

[I've gone out of orbit. I haven't the will.]

You have my will. You have to come home to hasten the climax of your disappearance. The scene is set, waiting for the masterstroke: the tearlashed apology, the small-fisted anger, the quick smoothing of a fresh sheet on the bed, the jerky embrace, the long stretching into blank sleep. Remember time. The perfect moment will disappear if you don't snatch it. Don't wait until my anger turns to dull despair. Come home now, now.

[You're sure another hour . . .]

Another hour at four beers per hour and your wrathful husband will be vomiting in the woody pine toilet bowl. You have to come now, with all deliberate speed.

[All right. I'm coming now.]

Goodnight, Blondie.

[Goodnight, Danny-boy.]

It's not just mind reading, you see, it's mind control, mind power, a mechanism of interpersonal relations. I have complete faith in it, complete confidence that I'll hear her footsteps in fifteen minutes. And why shouldn't she come home? She couldn't choose a detergent without me, no less a lover.

I feel bold enough to walk outside on the street and wait for her, but still I execute caution. If on the off-chance that I haven't reached her at all but simply contacted part of my own mind, and she doesn't come home . . . I might start howling in the street. Yes, it's safer sitting here staring into the sleepbitten face of brother Roger, waiting until I have concrete sensory proof that she has come. Meanwhile, I feel a lot better.

6

What do I take in my coffee? What does Allegra dream about? Who am I? What's my favorite number? What's that smell? Do I take sugar in my coffee? Why do I want to know? I'm glad I'm alone so I can have a lot of free time to unravel these, and other, questions. I said, I'm glad I'm alone. Roger's asleep in the ashtray. I feel sorry enough for you to cover you, Roger. His cheek twitches while he sleeps. I'm going to lie back and take a rest. I don't care if there is no sheet. I'll just throw a blanket over . . . a blanket over Roger, a blanket over the mattress, and no blanket for over me. I'll use my coat. So resourceful. I'll slip into a tub of oily flowery mother-of-pearl cream sauce sleep.

Bump. Scuffle. Shapes by the window. Scuffle. Fright in the night. Sigh. Is that the dream, beating its wings by the window? A colored dream perched like a tropical bird at the edge of my mind. I can catch a glimpse in my peripheral vision but as I turn my face towards it all I see are scarlet wings vanishing into a blue sky.

[Quiet, dear.]
Mama.
[Sweet dreams, dear.]
Mama, I never have sweet dreams anymore.
[You just don't remember them. Settle down, now.]
Tell me something. Tell me a story or a sing-song. I remember all my dreams. The worst nightmares happen when I'm awake. Tell me a story. What do you dream about, Mama? Tell me your favorite dream.
[Once I dreamt I was a teabag.]

Ha!

[It was a wonderful dream.]

Well—tell me.

[It was just a short dream. I was a teabag nestled in a box with rows of other teabags. I could see the white of a counter and someone moving about with a white apron on. I heard a man say Tea, please. Suddenly I was plucked up by my paper tag and plunked into a wide-mouthed cup. I was apprehensive. Then a splash. A cadenza of boiling water cascading over me. A giant realization of myself as the tea oooozed out of me in lovely orange streams swirling through the water. Then a fast dunk or two, a sharp squeeze against a spoon, and I landed in the saucer. Old, dried out, but terribly happy.]

I wonder what a Freudian would—

[Nonsense, dear.]

You haven't heard yet.

[I know it will be nonsense, dear. Close your eyes. How do you expect to sleep with your eyes bolt open?]

I've lost my eyelids.

[Danny. Yawn. Stretch. Curl up. Stretch out. Sigh deeply. Close your eyes. Sleep. It's nice to sleep. Ahhh.]

Not alone.

[You need your sleep.]

I thought I was drunk enough.

[Sleep is the best medicine.]

O sleep, gentle sleep, nature's soft nurse. Tell me another dream to dream, Mommy.

[Silence might be best.]

I never know silence. If you go away my mind will babble up another someone.

[My dreams are so usual. I dream about searching and searching for drapery hooks in a department store. Your father is waiting outside tapping his foot. The salesladies vanish as soon as I approach and—]

Mother! No anxiety dreams. I have enough of those.

[Well. Sometimes I have dreams without people in them. Very objective. Close your eyes. The other night I dreamt about a hat I once had when I was a girl. A red straw hat with wooden cherries on the brim. The hat was being carried slowly by the wind, blown down an empty street at first, past parked cars and empty store windows, then blown across a sand beach, out over the waves, then . . . that was all. It seemed significant. The hat represented my mind, I thought, my poor mind being blown about by the wind.]

I understand that. My mind. It's all I have left, you see. I wouldn't want to lose it. You can't take these things for granted. Allegra . . .

[Or the hat could be my youth passing me by. Close your eyes.]

I heard footsteps! I swear! ALLEGRA!!!!! Get the hell up here.

[If those were Allegra's footsteps, she's gained a hundred pounds. I heard a door close.]

Ah. The cop. The heavy-footed downstairs cop who lives next door to Roger. How late is it if he's coming home? We usually go to bed when he leaves for work. Oh God. Oh God. What do you dream about, Mama?

[I'd like to talk to her, let me tell you. I'd have a few choice words.]

How do you know? Who are you, voice of my mother? The last thing I would do is expose my wife to you! The very last thing.

[Are you always like that with Allegra? You must frighten her—she's so timid.]

Timid? The only thing in the world she's afraid of is you, Mama. There's nothing I haven't tried. There are no solutions I haven't thought of.

[You should be gentle and compassionate. . . .]

I'm not the type.

[Don't tell me what type you are. When you were a kid—]

I was great! I was really a terrific kid. I remember it well. But not now.

[When she comes home, don't let her apologize. Don't threaten. Just make her promise that she won't do it again. Make her reaffirm her wedding vow, say it again, out loud, before God, that she is yours alone, that she will obey you, whatever else you want. She'll do it. She'd be lucky to get off so easily, she'll think. You wouldn't be angry, remember, you wouldn't ask questions. Just a promise.]

Even if she did it she could break it, especially if she made it insincerely.

[Words have a power of their own. Once the pledge is made it becomes as solid as a building in your mind. It's harder to break the pledge than to keep it. The vow grows stronger each time temptation is resisted. It becomes stronger than any desire to break it. It would be better if it was sincere, of course, but an insincere pledge is better than none. How many times did we force you to say I'm sorry when you weren't sorry? Each time the power of the words took over until you were indeed sorry and made your own silent vow not to smoke cigarettes or talk fresh or whatever. And you understood this when you were a child. If you really thought you were unjustly blamed we couldn't make you say I'm sorry. You were a beautiful child.]

The curse of a happy childhood. What could possibly happen now to make me as happy as I was then? It makes me tremble. If all my wishes were granted—I still wouldn't be happy. Will you wither away if I get a divorce, Mother?

[As far as I'm concerned, Danny, your life is settled. We have other troubles now. There's your brother. It's his turn to want to quit school. He says he's not at all worried about the draft, even though the Mendle, New Hampshire, draft board has never granted a classification of conscientious objector. I'd rather rot in jail than rot in school, he says. He's such a big talker. Would you write to him?]

Dear Steven, In my opinion all this tough talk is just meant to make me look bad. Have you heard the latest news? All men between the ages of eighteen and thirty-six who refuse to fight in Vietnam will face a firing squad at noon tomorrow. What are your plans? Will you go kill Vietcong, hoping they won't get you, or march toward a heroic, but certain, death? Isn't the new law wonderful? We'll know for sure whether we're pacifists or cowards. P.S. Academic life is not so bad. At last week's peace demonstration we rampaged in the streets to the wonderful sound of crashing glass. P.P.S. I wanted you to be the first to know that Allegra and I have split up. Can you fix me up with Kitty Purdue over Christmas?

[Be as callous as you want. I've managed to stand all the other heartache you and your brother have given me.]

Well, goodnight, Mother; nice of you to drop in.

[Remember, what's right for all of us is what's right for you. You're part of a family. You were such a beautiful child. Those precious years when you didn't know there were at least two sides to every question.]

So you've been here and I haven't gone to sleep and I still don't know what to do.

[Ask *her* family. I raised *you*, not her. *I* did my job well. *You're* home in bed where you belong, aren't you?]

Come again, Mother. This was most interesting. I'll call you. But you won't be able to hear, will you? There's company downstairs.

[Goodnight, dear.]

You're going to leave me alone. Is there company downstairs? I'll never fall asleep! Why are you going away when you know I can't fall asleep? Send the company home.

[What more do you want? I've told you two stories, you've had your glass of water, your goodnight kisses, your blankets tucked just so. Goodnight.]

Goodnight! It's always goodnight! That's all you ever really said to me. Goodnight, dear.

[Goodnight, my dear, sleep tight, and dream sweet, my dear.]

Say that again. God, I can never quite control these voices. Say it again. Goodnight . . . Three times is good luck. Say it three times, Mother. Goodnight . . . I'll never fall asleep. I'll stay up until they all go home. When she comes up to check on me I'll be staring at the ceiling with tears on my cheeks. She'll be sorry she left me when she knew I couldn't fall asleep. I'm not the least bit tired. And I'm so weary of dreaming.

[There are people downstairs! Our friends. I'm not going to let your mother spend the evening up here with you, do you understand? You're a big boy now.]

I can't fall asleep.

[You do this on purpose. Every time we have company. If it weren't for your mother I'd—]

Oh yeah? When I'm president I'll do whatever I want! I'll stay up all night and make everyone else stay up with me. When I'm president—

[Humph, don't forget about pressure groups.]

I never get to do anything I want! Everyone else can do their homework at night. Everyone else's allowed to read comic books.

[But not everyone will be president of the United States. You settle down now.]

Neither will I. No matter what Mommy says. Boy, if you want to get a lot of laughs at school, just say you're going to be president when you grow up. Who ever heard of a president from New Hampshire? How much longer will I have to go to school?

[Do you hear them laughing downstairs? Sandy Richler is telling another funny story and I missed it. Goodnight, kid.]

Just tell me a short one. I promise I'll shut up.

[When I was a kid. When I was a kid. When I was just about as young as you are now.]

How long ago was that, Daddy?

[Long, long before you were born, in the time of the Great Depression.]

There wasn't any United Nations.

[No.]

You didn't have any toys?

[We made them ourselves! We made them out of string, shirtboard, flour, and water.]

What's shirtboard, Daddy?

[Humph, try to go to sleep, Danny. I'll send your mother up in a little while.]

I think I dozed off for a minute. I was standing out in space watching the earth turn. My vision penetrated the crust of the globe where I could see thousands of eyeballs rolling about in coffins. The eyeballs were as hard as marbles. They rattled when the earth turned.

It's worth staying up to avoid a dream like that. The cursed immortality, to keep on seeing after death, to watch the generations repeat your mistakes.

Smells like she left the oven on from this morning.

This pea coat is short. I can't take back the blanket I gave Roger. I can't sleep on top of the pea coat and use . . . I can pull half this cover over me, leaving half under, ah. Not too bad if I don't move and I hold myself very straight.

I'm going to pressure the city council to allow one all-night bar. I'll form a group to represent the temporarily insane. People Under Stress. We'll jam the council meeting and show them how upset we are. Insomniacs need a meeting place.

And when I'm elected I won't forget the kookie brothers and sisters who gave unstintingly of their time and anxiety.

And when I'm elected I promise to free all of you from your pasts, provide free therapy for your children, and . . . there's always supposed to be three promises. An all-night bar in every town.

[If you come to my bar I'll put you in touch with some fine people. Men who know how to drink and feel good about it. And not only does it stay open quite late, but it's crowded, and there's always a fight on Friday night. Remember last Christmas I took Allegra and you by there. And that was an off-night. Most of the regulars were with their families, Christmas Eve and all.]

Ask her family. But I didn't ask. Are these voices inviting each other now?

[Tell me, what do you think the big bastard's doing in Vietnam now, Danny?]

Bending at the elbow, he faces me with the width of his arm and shoulder raised as if he were playing defensive end. Uninvited guests in the middle of the night. I'll just pretend I'm asleep.

[What I'm trying to say is, in the sixty-four election one bastard says he'll bomb them over there, the other bastard says he won't. You know which one won. You know what he did. You even voted for him yourself, Danny, your first time voting. So now I'm down at Dirty Mary's discussing politics and I'd like to pick some opinions out of your brain so when I shoot my mouth off I sound like something.]

Go away.

[Last Christmas you told me that stuff about balance of payments and devaluation of the dollar. . . . I used that for months. I was Dirty Mary's *authority* on "our monetary policy." Help me out again, Danny. I work all day. I'm a slow reader. What about those kids burning their draft cards? Some fella in here is saying all those kids are faggots who are afraid to fight for their country. Now I can just strut up and say, Oh you bastard, my son-in-law is no faggot and he ain't afraid of shit! He's only a little guy like me, I could punch him out. But I'd kind of rather say some sharp things to him first: Why, you old fool, don't you understand that it's different today? It's not like our war. Our war was worth something. It has nothing to do with them being afraid. Are you going to let me flounder around like this? Take pity on an old drunk, Danny. Give me some of your flashy words.]

I'm only interested in myself tonight.

[Well I'll be a son-of-a-fuckin'-bitch.]

I'm worrying about your daughter.

[I heard something worth repeating tonight. This big-mouth sounded pretty good until he got going on draft dodgers. Ah yes: If you want to see how straight your course is, look to your wake.]

Is that a piece of advice?

[An old sailor's saw.]

O.k., thanks, I'll think it over. My wake is zigzagged and crisscrossed and marking a giant circle. I guess I'm in trouble.

[Well, aren't we all.]

I need advice. As long as you're here. How should I handle her? Certainly you faced the problem in the past yourself.

[I wouldn't use the word "faced," Danny. It's a bit strong. Every time Allegra brought one of her dates into the house I'd be sure not to be there. Every time she came home at four a.m. I'd be sure to be sound asleep. Let her mother make chatty conversation with all the young men. No reason for me to try to be civil to them. Or to you. Politics is the only proper conversation to have with a son-in-law.]

If you'd been stricter. If you'd given her some sort of a moral code. Any moral code.

[Maybe she would be different. But better? She'd be like everyone else. She's not an assembly-line girl. She was always a pirate. From the time she was little, if you mentioned something she shouldn't do you could just see her eyes skipping over the moments until she *could* play with matches, hold the cat by the tail, lean very very very far out the window. I didn't form her, but I didn't try to change her. I knew that someday a sucker like you would take her off my hands. She's just like me. She can't tolerate the slightest bit of discipline. Of course I've learned.]

You didn't form her. But she's exactly like you. Are you saying it's just a coincidence? A family infection?

[You can out-argue me any day, buddy, but I can still tell you a few things you don't know.]

I like you. I've always liked you. I can't understand why you're so hostile towards me.

[The man my daughter chose. It must rile every father if she doesn't choose a copy of himself. And if she does, the mother screams, Haven't you learned a thing living with your father, girl? You're crazy to marry another drunken bum like your father! But she didn't. She married you. Maybe you were the first to ask her.]

I guess I was.

[Well that in itself can sway a woman. Now Allegra's mother didn't marry until she was pushing thirty, and although we marry later in Norway, I'm sure she had her moments of wondering if she'd die a virgin. Not that that was ever Allegra's problem. A mother like that has fears for her daughter. You got to get married young, Allegra, real young. And even so I'll be dead before you give me a grandchild.]

Do you think it would help if we had a kid?

[Help what? I think it would be great!]

Help Allegra settle down.

[The fine art of conversation is obviously dying. All people want to talk about is their personal problems. The truth is there's no such thing as problems. Things happen to you. Some almost kill you. Others are not so bad. They're not fancy equations to be solved.]

You're confusing me. What should I do? Just lie back and let things roll over me?

[Do what you feel like doing. When I'm miserable I don't feel like lying on a crumpled blanket with a pea coat over my chest. My God, you've gotten *me* depressed. I'm just about to swing the conversation in Dirty Mary's around to my son-in-law's fancy problems. Allegra's been running away since she was eleven.]

Why did she run away?

[I guess she had someplace she wanted to go. Or didn't like where she was. No particular reason that I ever noticed.]

Was she beautiful then?

[Between eleven and fifteen she looked like a red-headed mishap. Her arms were so long she could touch the floor without bending over. Did you hear they expect we'll have three hundred thousand troops over there by the end of the year? I don't understand what they have on their minds. The men at work think we should either beat them to hell or get the hell out.]

Tell me what to do.

[I'm going to get drunker and try to forget this conversation, I tell you.]

Not in my mind you don't! You stay here until I dismiss you.

[May I please be dismissed?]

First tell me what to do. Tell me!

[Drop dead. Eat a horse. Get a mistress. Quit school and get acquainted with honest labor. Eat a peanut butter and jelly sandwich.]
Say!
[Take up knitting.]
Would you like a peanut butter and jelly sandwich?
[So long.]

I am getting hungry. One more try at sleep and then I'll give up. Relax your toes. How can you relax your toes with your socks on? Take your socks off. That's a lot better. Relax your insteps. Relax your heels. Relax your ankles. Relax your calves. Calves! Tense your calves, one, two, three, four, relax. Relax your thighs. Relax your legs. They'll never move again. Feel that tingle? Skin feels good. If I could move my legs I'd take my pants off.

7

The phone's ringing. The phone is actually ringing! This is no fantasy. The loudest sound in the world. Black brain jangling. I can't move.

I said, I can't move. My legs are stuck together. Is that the third ring? My hands are stuck to my sides. My body has evaporated. I think I can move my tongue.

Roger! Oh, there he goes, leaping out of the tray of ashes.

—ello. Yeah. Yeah. I'll tell him.

You've heard that one about the tree falling in the forest when there's no one around to hear it. Did it really make a sound? Is Roger talking to himself? Are they talking about the tree?

—I'll get him. Yeah, I understand. No, this is Roger. Roger Falik, I met you at their wedding. Will you hold on?

It must be for me. I can't get up.

—Yer wanted on the phone, Dan. They caught her.

—Who?

—Allegra. Her parents snatched her up at Kennedy airport.

—In New York?

—They're holding on. Why are you lying there like a stiff wrapped in your pea coat?

—I can't get up, Roger. My body is paralyzed. I have no sensation below my tongue. Don't look at me that way. Just go back and tell them I'm . . . out looking for Allegra. Tell them I heard there was an auto accident on College and Market and went to check it out. I'll explain later. You gotta do it for me, Roger. We're fraternity brothers, right? Go ahead . . . No, I really can't move any part of my body. Even my face is frozen in this grin. I know I sound calm about it. Go ahead. You're a good friend, Roger. Get the whole story, will you?

I guess it is true. I can't move my feet. I can't even feel my feet. This is the worst. First I couldn't fall asleep, now I can't get up. The room is crowded with sunlight.

—He's not in right now, he's out looking for her.

He's a great friend. Roger . . . what can I do for you, Roger? Get Allegra to cook dinner for him more often. Kennedy airport? Fix him up with a nice girl.

—I'm not sure I'm following this. Would you mind going over it again, Mrs. Nyland? I see. Wait a moment, I think I hear Danny coming in now. Would you hold on again?

Betrayed? I'll make one effort. Move body, leap. No, I cannot move a fingernail towards that phone. If the phone were near the bed he could hold it to my ear.

—Dan, they're gonna put her away. For thirty days. Her family doctor suggested a voluntary commitment. She's willing, supposedly. Do you want to stop it? I'll pull the bed near the phone. Do you want to talk?

—That's all right, Roger, you're doing fine. Just say it wasn't me you heard.

—It's me again, Mrs. Nyland. Nah, it wasn't him. I'll have him call you later. Can I talk to Allegra? Oh, I see. Well, tell her hello when she quiets down. Do what you think is best. Yes, I'm sure you're thinking of her best interests. Thanks for calling and all.

—You did great, Roger.

—You juvenile piece of shit.

—I really can't move. I don't even feel uncomfortable.

—I'm going to stick this safety pin into you if you don't . . .

—Go on, I'm curious myself.

—Don't you feel this? Danny, you really don't feel this?

—Try sticking it in my arms. My legs are goners.

—That's incredible. Let me try it on myself . . . ouch! This pin is sharp. How can you not feel it?

—Try my face. Are you doing it hard?

—There's blood spots when I take it out.

—I feel something in the lower part of my face. Yes, I think I felt that. I guess my face is only partly numb.

—I'm going to sit on your legs. Don't tell me you can't feel my weight.

—I can't feel your weight. I hate to sound impatient, Roger, but would you mind telling me what Allegra's mother had to say?

—Oh. Well, our friend Allegra has been on a big adventure. She left Candle City this morning and flew to Chicago.

From Chicago she took a plane to St. Louis, then rushed to catch the very next flight back to Chicago where she took another airline to Denver. I think I'm getting this straight. She called her parents collect from Denver to say she was moving on to San Francisco because the Denver airport was full of turkeys. Then she called them collect from San Francisco to say the turkeys had followed her and she thought Mexico would be a more humane environment. Then she flew from Mexico City back to Chicago with the idea of coming back here to talk it over with you, but instead she flew to Kennedy and called her parents to say she had eluded the turkeys and was waiting for an eleven-o'clock plane for Jamaica because it's a million miles from winter and just a few dollars from home. So they drove out to Kennedy and with the aid of two policemen and their family doctor took her over to the nearest mental hospital, where she voluntarily committed herself for thirty days. It's hard to say what "voluntarily" means, though. When I asked to talk to her, Mrs. Nyland said she was screaming about turkeys and couldn't come to the phone.

Roger is leaning over me as he says this. He sounds bored with the whole story.

—Where'd she get the money for the planes?

—Yeah, that's the clincher. She used your credit card. I thought that would make you sit up in bed, Dan, but I guess your paralysis act is here to stay. What's that smell? Ugh, you left this pot in the oven all night. It's burnt to hell.

—The poor kid. A mental hospital. She always said she'd go crazy.

—They said she screamed, kicked, and clawed when they took her from the airport.

—She always did like flying.

—You're in this thing together, aren't you? She goes flying around nuts, you go nuts in bed, and my job is to answer the phone and run errands.

—If I could move, I'd pat your arm in appreciation, Roger.

—Let me pull your bed over to the phone, 'cause I have to leave for class soon.

—I'm o.k. where I am. I couldn't lift my arm to get the phone anyway. Later you should get someone from student health to come over. Much later. I want to see if it goes away. Once before when I was hung over I lost some sensation in my legs and the feeling came back in an hour.

—I think you're in it together. I'm feeling sick. Yoder, you got thirty days where you won't have to wonder where your wife is. Are you just gonna stay in bed?

—Thanks for everything, Roger. When are you coming back?

—After class, I guess. If my stomach can take it. I'll bring you some franks and beans.

—Bring cigarettes, Roger. You're a great friend. Next month I'm going to be your best friend.

8

And yet there was a time when the sun shone for me, the snow flaked to give my sled cutting, the rain fell to give me time to read my comic books. Every morning I woke up bright and healthy like yellow banana slices floating in fresh cold milk.

I love this room. The dresser with a stocking snagging out of an open drawer. On top of the dresser is one of our better piles. Linen . . . well, I'll be . . . is that a sheet right up there? If I had noticed that last night I could have put it on the bed. I might not be paralyzed now if I hadn't spent the night in a blanket sandwich with a pea coat on my chest. Linen, notebooks, schoolbooks, telephone book sliding off the side, newspapers piled up in front of the mirror. Dangling beads. Lemon-lime after-shave lotion without a cap. Three alarm clocks. It is now nine thirty. It is now nine thirty. It is now nine thirty. This is the longest she's ever been gone. How many minutes in thirty days' absence? I love our junk. She's gone away and left me all the junk.

I still can't feel my body. Roger covered me before he left, and though I see the long line of my body under the ash-colored blanket, I feel like a disembodied head on a pillow. My heart must be working or I wouldn't be alive, right? My lungs, my kidneys. Will I feel it when I have to urinate? It doesn't matter. In my case my body is vestigial.

Allegra. Leggie? Legs? Who told you you could go any-where? On my credit card. Oh God, on my mother's credit card.

[Make 'em pay.]

How much was it? Did you save the charge slips?

[Threw 'em away.]

A fine mess. You should have called me. Why didn't you call me instead of your parents?

[Danny, I was never more than a figleaf of your imagi-nation. There's no hope for a mind that's lost its message and meandered . . .]

I'll never recover from this. This is worse than the time Regina Cumberland told me she loved me.

[What are you lying there for? I expected to see you pacing around smoking cigarettes.]

I don't want to upset you further, Allegra. But the truth is I'm paralyzed. Last night I couldn't fall asleep because I was worrying about you. So I did that part-by-part relaxation and put my body to sleep. Well, it's still asleep, but my mind is rampaging the cosmos in search of you.

[Where thoughts flip through faster than a fall frolic and the meanings are not clear.]

It's not your fault, Allegra. I am fully paralyzed. Roger stuck a safety pin into my arms, my legs, my chest. He kept sticking it in, angrily, but I didn't feel it. I cannot move my big toe. I don't feel stiff, or numb; I don't feel anything.

[It's another figleaf of your imagination. You never could feel anything, Danny. Not even excitement.]

That was your department. You sure monopolized the excitement last night. While I waited for you, growing number and number. What were you doing flying all over the country? Who told you you could go anywhere?

[I resent that. I didn't fly "all over the country." I flew from place to place. I was always going somewhere. I'd still be on my way if they hadn't . . . They have very good water fountains at airports. I miss them. The water here is lukewarm in paper cups that smell like medicine bottles. At the airport they have a shiny chrome water fountain. I couldn't get over the confidence of those people; the way they just stood up, bent over for a drink, then licked their lips as if no one was watching. My throat was fuzzy under my nearly nude lipstick. I decided to risk standing way up on my high-heeled boots. This was at O'Hare airport. My stockings didn't puff at the knees. Worth the dollar ninety-eight for that bit of security in an insecure world. World. The red plush carpet curved like the earth towards the fountain. I plunged in my nearly nude lips. The water was cold; it made my teeth metal. I kept drinking, torturing my gums, drinking, drinking until my chest filled up with air gulped down to my stomach which started to puff out against my black knit dress. I drank until I was afraid everyone was watching me drink so long. I bumped my lips against a tissue before turning to face my audience:

[A row of Chicago businessmen: crewcut turkeys with shaved chins overhanging tight collars. Pretending to read a newspaper. Joking with each other. One young one whose chin didn't hang over winked at me. A loud crash of a wink.

[A row of San Francisco men in sunglasses. In white pants. The same water fountain. Green print shirts. The same red plush carpet curving up the way the world curves. He took off his sunglasses and set them down on his movie script: Hi there. You're on now. Pivot on the carpet. Slowly now. That's it. Perfect. I felt my nylons slipping.

[A row of American ladies down in Mexico for divorces, sighing in teary relief. They're all on camera. The turkeys waddle on the plush red carpet. Their heads jerk from girl to girl. Red gargleous adam's apples gulping, squawking eeuwell eeuwell. Profiles: one black, blinkless eye. Mexicans are the loudest lookers. They all have webbed feet. My stockings are ringing around my ankles.

[I didn't have to sit there. I was free. I ran up the granite ramps, around the concrete globes resting on cylinders, past the arrows, and over the gray mosaic floors. I kept away from the luggage racks. I had no luggage. Those suitcases on the circling bands reminded me of a lab experiment where rats snatch bits of food off a revolving table. I kept far away from the luggage area. That was a firm policy.

[I ran along an expanse of blue wall with letters as high as I am: rest rooms, refreshments. The airport stretches further than the eye can see in all directions. The Muzak is so tranquil it makes my arms float up from my sides, while my mind flies off around the expanse of the airport which stretches further than the ears can hear.

[The travel bar has a wall of black, white, silver checks moving up and down diagonally. The silver checks are mirrors reflecting more black, white, and silver checks moving in diagonal rows. It's dark in the bar. Close. You can only see a few yards ahead. The wood is polished. Glasses tinkle with low laughter. The bar Muzak is livelier. A female voice sings pop-pops about love. A St. Louis man with his face lined with smiles buys me a drink and leans on me. He's not heavy. He leans lightly. He does the smiling so I don't have to.

["Passengers for flight one-ninety-two to Denver should now be ready for boarding at gate twelve." I have time for one more drink but I won't miss my flight for him. Business before pleasure. I tell him about my husband who's going to be president. I have no money left. It's a good thing I'm getting a meal flight. "Passengers for flight one-ninety-two to Denver should now be on board." Running down past gates two, six, eight . . . I was the last one to board that flight. I took a seat between two turkeys: two profiles with black eyes looking at me sideways. One kept his eye on my knee and the crease of my thigh. The other eye stared at the tip of my breast, except when I crossed my high-heeled boots knee over knee.

[The plane rolled forward slowly. We waited for another plane to take off. There was a roar of engines. I closed my eyes for the gentle lift up and up, circling with wing tipped towards the city lights, rising over the globe, up like a sigh.

[There were some bumps on that flight. The worst weather was flying to New York. Lightning flashed near the plane. We dipped suddenly and my cold coffee spilled on the hem of my dress. That's when I decided to fly to Jamaica to dry off and warm up. I think I would have liked Jamaica. I was reading a newspaper on the plane, a week-old New York newspaper. How can I put this? I wasn't really reading it. The plane was bumping. The man who was sitting next to me changed seats so I could get a better look at the lightning, and so he could throw up over the aisle. I had this old New York newspaper . . . what's that noise, Danny? I can't think with all that noise.]

My phone is ringing.

[Well, get it.]

I can't move my body out of the bed to answer the phone. It's probably your parents calling back. That's the fourth ring. I hate that sound, yet my ears strain to listen to the iiiiing. I can feel the sound up and down my spine.

[That's a good sign, Daniel. You're recovering from the shock. Please get up and answer the phone like a good boy. Your father and I are very anxious to talk to you.]

Go away, Mother. I'm paralyzed.

[We just spoke to Allegra's mother and she's so upset. Everyone is upset.]

That's the sixth ring, Mother; would you mind hanging up?

[You said you were feeling it in your spine. I know you're going to recover very soon, Daniel. You have resiliency. We all do in this family. When you were a child, I always told you there are things in life we don't like but we have to face them anyway.]

Hang up, Mother.

[This is a serious matter. We're all very concerned. Allegra is obviously unsettled. And so irresponsible about money . . .]

That's ten rings. Here comes eleven . . . no . . . a ring of silence. My body dissolves into transparency again. Rest. A thousand miles away and they still intrude whenever they like.

[I was telling you about flying to New York.]

Go on.

[The plane was bumping up and down. I had an old newspaper folded open on my lap. The lights blinked off for a moment and I heard the man next to me retching. When the lights came on I was staring at "D'Angelo, Anthony, 1201 Burke Avenue, Bronx, New York: killed in action." There were a lot of other names. It was the honor roll of Vietnam war dead. Tony D'Angelo stepped on a land mine forty miles north of Saigon. Tony was the ice-cream man who offered me forty dollars to go in the bushes with him. I ran all the way home.]

I'm sorry that happened to him, Allegra.

[Yeah. I felt . . . I felt the war was real.]

Stinking war. Our generation deserves a better war.

[I looked out the plane window. I could see them bombing Cleveland.]

I wonder how it really feels to be in it. I wonder if I would have been brave or . . .

[Oh, you would have. You always win medals; it's your style. You wouldn't have been able to disappoint your sergeant. But Tony D'Angelo was probably sneaking off to visit a girl when the lightning flashed in the final dissolve.]

I'm sorry about Tony. Leggie—are you aching with world vision and global connections? What did you see flying around up there?

[I saw them bombing Cleveland. I saw . . . this hospital gown gapes open in the back, letting the cold air chill my spine. I get scared when I see the connections zagging over me and under me but never through me. *I'm* the one who will never know. Oh, the contempt I used to feel for you and Roger and Frank Lesser as you discussed ancient and modern ways of evading the draft. I felt so superior to you. Wouldn't I have found a better way than marching to an easy death, or dying of an easy life? I'd sit there watching your adam's apples gargling up your shaven necks. I'd drink the beers down twice as fast as you guys because I didn't have anything to say. Why didn't I ever get to face a historic decision? I wish they'd tried to draft me! I resent not being asked. Forced to fight all my wars with you.]

You're lucky not to have to make historic decisions. You're outside history, Allegra; you transcend history.

[Sitting there, getting drunker, listening to Frank Lesser tell how his great-great-grandfather shot off his trigger finger to escape the Tsarist army. Sitting there for years and years with nothing to say. Once in a while you'd turn to me and say, You look terrif tonight, Allegra.]

You are great-looking, Allegra. Allegra? The phone again. You should enjoy the luxury of being adored, Allegra. Allegra?

[What do you think the big bastard will do over there now, Danny?]

Leggie? Legs?

[I just heard a report that US casualties for the month of October—]

Go away, Mr. Nyland. I'm talking to Allegra. I'm not going to pick up the phone.

[—listen to these numbers, Danny; you're supposed to be so brilliant. Do you believe it? They say we lost fifty-three men, with five hundred and sixteen South Vietnamese soldiers killed and two thousand, five hundred and twenty-one enemy casualties. Now bigmouth at the bar here says those figures show we're winning. We're slaughtering them. Killing more of them every day. He says you gotta add the South to the North Viets and . . . I forget how his argument . . . It don't matter whether they're from the South or the North, the more that get killed the better. Come on now, Dan, a few fancy words for me to flash in his face.]

I said the wrong thing to her. She mixes me up. If I don't compliment her enough she gets riled, but God forbid I should compliment her at the wrong moment when she wants to hear how sensitive or intelligent she is. . . . I'm feeling those telephone rings between my toes. It's so weird. A head, a space, a tickle between the toes.

[What are you saying, Dan?]

They make up those casualty figures, of course! The entire war could be a fantasy as far as I know. It's all in my mind, isn't it? Nothing outside my mind really matters, does it? If I didn't turn on the t.v. or the five-o'clock news I wouldn't even know they had a war today. If you didn't keep dropping in to remind me! What are you after, Mr. Nyland?

[I've always been impressed by you college types.]

Tell me what happened to Allegra. Was it a bad scene at the airport? Only four rings? Is this another pause between? No. Only four rings. Thank you. They're beginning to understand. Soon they'll all stop calling.

This room with its piles of junk. Don't you want to come back to our stuff, Allegra? You can't leave me with all this. Let's start over again. Are you aching with world vision, Allegra? How did you think it up? Flying all over the country.

[I told you—I was always going somewhere.]

Leggie, I'm so glad you're back. I'm sorry . . .

[This is our last conversation, Danny-baby. She heard me talking to myself. She gave me pills to quiet me down. I'm going to forget all about you.]

As soon as I recover from the shock, Allegra. I'm going to fly straight to—

[It wasn't your fault, Danny.]

Ha.

[You're the perfect husband. Believe me, you are. I was never going to get married. But then there you were. Tall, intelligent, athletic, talky-talky on any subject. A bit of a fuck-up in college. I thought that was a nice touch.]

As soon as I can get up I'm going to fly to New York and visit you. I'm going to bring you oily flowery bath oil and violet stockings.

[No! You won't be able to crash this place. No turkeys or relatives allowed. I asked them *that* before I signed up. I stopped screaming long enough to check *that* out. This place is a hospital, not a zoo.]

They call it a hospital? I thought it would be Miss Miller's Home for Wayward Girls or something.

[I don't know what Miss Miller calls it. She hasn't said a word to me that didn't end in a question. When I got here she unzipped my high-heeled boots and rolled off my black stockings with three runs zigging up from the right ankle. She washed the sting of honey-bee lipstick off my mouth with a brown paper. I knew it was a hospital because of the rough paper towels. I wasn't kicking after that. After she took off my boots I stopped kicking. She patted my head. She gave me a nice starchy hospital gown. It ties around the waist and gapes open in the back. I have it on right now. She's going to let me keep it. My body is sighing under it. I don't miss my perishable clothes. My breasts clang freely together. I see my arms are gripped by black-and-blue policeman fingerprints. My thighs are rippling naked. I'm going to forget all about you.

[I never even wanted a perfect husband. I told her that. But it's like turning down a million dollars. Here—here's a free million dollars, no strings attached. Now you know there must be strings attached. You're not that stupid. But dazzle razzle a million dollars. A perfect husband. Handsome too. What more could a girl? Great career ahead of him. And he wants you. Come with me and be my love. Never have to worry about where your next box of valentine chocolates are coming from. A lifetime of love. I promise! Oh, there must be a string attached somewhere. A million dollars, a perfect husband, all the chocolate you can eat . . . because he fell in love with YOU.

[The string dangled down my throat. I kept trying to cough it up but I'd gag and have to swallow it again. I was gagging while she weighed and measured me. She put her cold fingers around the base of my neck and slowly slowly squeezed her fingers closer until my tongue hung out making toilet bowl sounds. The string came up. I held it in my hand. She let go of my throat. I threw the string in the waste-

basket. I told her I didn't have a husband: I was just making up that stuff I told you before, Miss Miller. I wish I was married. Maybe if I'm lucky I'll get married someday. But no one has asked me yet. The answer pleased her immensely. She gave me a cigarette and lit it. I'm going to forget all about you.]
I'm crazier than you, Allegra. I'm crazier than you'll ever be! Any woman who can have orgasms is not crazy! Let me in there! We're in this thing together. I can't forget about you. You're my anima. You're the dark half of the moon. I'm crazier. I talk to myself. I admit that. Tell them you have a husband who talks to himself. I can't make decisions. I can't function. Tell them I can't even—
[Your phone is ringing.]
You see? I can't even move my body out of this bed to answer the phone.
[Only women can have nervous breakdowns—by definition.]
Ask Roger how crazy I am. I wouldn't let him sleep all night. You're not crazy, Allegra. You've always been an extremist.
[I'm allowed to act crazier than you, Danny. I'm outside history, right? I have to make my own history.]
That's the fourth ring. I hate that sound. Allegra—you managed to fly all around the country; to coolly get your credit card stamped, make reservations, decide to leave town again and again . . .
[A lot of people are crazier than I am, Danny. You gotta have a gimmick.]
The phone is ringing between my toes and behind my knees. A few sensations wiggling up to the disembodied head. No one will ever make the bed like you, Allegra. Too hot to touch. I'll never forget about you. I'll remember you slugging bourbon into your mouth so hard . . . remember the

night we were drinking with Roger and Frank Lesser and you slugged the bourbon into your mouth so hard that the glass hit your gums. And when you slammed it back on the table it had blood around the rim. What a turn-on. Blood arcing around the tops of your teeth. Hang up the damn phone, Mother. I was looking for a girl like you, Allegra. Stretched out like the earth, hilly and smooth. Dozens of men could rest their heads on you and still feel lonely. Ten hands could nestle in your crotch and not fill you up. Ten tongues tangle in your mouth. Terrible to find what you're looking for.

I thought I had you fenced in with moral imperatives. You were invaded, conquered. Terrible to lose what you've always been looking for. Who told you you could leave town?

I haven't been counting the rings, Mother, but I'm sure that's more than ten. I don't have to stay married to her now, do I? Not after this.

[I don't think we can afford her, Daniel. We'll pay her medical bills, of course. No one will be able to say you drove her crazy and then left her. . . .]

I drove her crazy? She was demented from the moment I met her. She's crazier than I'll ever be. I'll never be president.

[Wipe that smirk off your face.]

She ruined my record.

[Can you feel your legs now? Why don't you try moving?]

I'll never be president. I can do whatever I want. Stop ringing the phone.

[You talk to him, Jay.]

[When I was a kid . . . When I was just about as old as you are now . . .]

My leg moved. It slid right off the bed.

[. . . I got arrested on a picket line . . .]

Was that in the Great Depression, Daddy?

[. . . and my mother said I'd ruined my record and would never be president, but my father said . . .]

I'm off the bed. I'm sitting on the brown braided rug with floppety arms.

[. . . my father said it was all right, I could still be a presidential adviser, and they were the ones who had the real power anyway.]

I didn't know you wanted to be president.

[The thing to remember about becoming a presidential adviser is, first you have to become an expert in some area like political structure or economics, or the relation of political structure to economics, and, second . . .]

I wonder if I can make it to the bathroom?

[. . . you have to know the president.]

Standing up with just one arm leaning on the sink. Pissing foam into the toilet bowl. Allegra always wished she could piss standing up. I remember the night Roger and I pissed over the railing into the Mississippi River. . . . Dad, maybe Roger should be president.

[Fine, fine.]

The phone stopped ringing. That must have been twenty rings. I can't fool them. They know I'm here. I guess I'll answer it next time. Presidential adviser on . . . figuring out who owns everything. Leave it to my dad to think that up. Roger *would* make a better president. He's always got a suntan. His father has lots of money. It feels good to move around again. I feel like I was never paralyzed. He's got a clean record. If you take my advice, Mr. President—may I still call you Roger?—you'll stop this war. Now, I know you didn't start it, and you've got to honor our commitments abroad, but this war is sapping our nation's strength. It's killing our roots, shriveling our leaves. *Who* said we should use the big bomb over there? You're not going to listen to some shit in a uniform, are you, Roger? He wasn't even in our fraternity. I have here my term paper on Political Theory which clearly shows that the US can maintain its world position by allowing selected revolutions to take place abroad while preventing any major change at home. I got an A on that paper, Roger; you gotta listen to me. O.k., I'll write you another memorandum. Yes, without footnotes this time.

I think I'll eat a bowl of crunchies with banana slices and cold milk. Now about the matter of political appointments, Roger, I must decline. Secretary of State is not for me. With my record I'll never get senate approval. Just keep me on as Special Presidential Assistant. You know there are still three members of our fraternity who have not been given appointments. Some very bright men, Roger, one of them is black, too, and that looks good. How about creating a special task force to study the problems of the mentally ill? Yes, I am still thinking about Allegra, poor thing. Such an unfortunate situation.

[I'm going to get cured, Danny. Rested up and released. You're going to hate me when I'm cured.]

You know, you don't look well today, Roger. You've been working so hard lately. I haven't seen you drunk since the night you were elected. Every time I pass the Oval Room at two, three, four in the morning I see the sunlamp still burning. How come *I'm* passing by at that hour? I try to do my share of the work, Mr. President. I don't want it all to fall on your oh-so-able shoulders. For old times' sake, let's take the night off, Roger. We'll call up Alice Little and Kitty Purdue. We'll put a case of beer in the trunk and drive out to the reservoir. How 'bout it, Roger? We'll have a great party.

GIRL-FRIENDS

Please understand
I never had a secret charm
To get me to the heart
of this or any other matter
—Leonard Cohen

1

I'm an odd sort of woman
Alone alone and I know why
I never seem to hold a man
And that's because I just won't try

He lowered his mouth onto hers, their tongues running together like two mountain streams. Zimmie leaned her head lightly on his shoulder, keeping the weight on her own neck, curbing her desire to slump on his shoulder. She was keeping the bruised feeling in and in, but there was a baby inside her too; there wasn't much room.

"Any last-minute instructions?"

Chopper rubbed his hands over her belly. "Don't have the baby till I get back."

"I mean what the hell am I supposed to do while you're meditating on the glories of nature?"

"Ah, Zimmie, you'll find things to do. You've been spending too much time hanging around to see what I'm going to do next. You admitted that yourself." He was bouncing in the heavy freedom of his hiking boots and thick socks, the pockets of his paratrooper jacket loaded down with canteen, books, and maps.

She felt like a pond after the boy took his sailboat and went home. She felt like a child whose mommy dropped her hand in the middle of traffic. She felt like screaming, What about *me*, why aren't you thinking of *me*?

Chopper hitched his pack onto his shoulders. Zimmie thought she could see a double highway with a white line down the middle of his face. "I hope it rains every day and you get a million mosquito bites," she said.

"You should have brought up these feelings before."

"I didn't have these feelings before!"

"Zimmie, I love being around you. I'll be back." He kissed her again, slowly, as if it would last all evening, then stepped off the porch and walked down the tree-edged street. She let him almost reach the corner, then shouted, "Don't abandon me!" and ran after him, belly bouncing, breasts swinging. A pack of children on bicycles stared at her.

Chopper laughed, waiting for her to catch up, and leaned his arm across her shoulders as they walked toward the highway. At least I made a scene, she thought, the bitterness dissolving for a moment. They reached Route 80, that flat white road with fields tipping off the gradings and semi-trucks roaring by in whirlwinds. He took out the *Colo.* sign she'd watched him crayon. He tucked his long blond hair under his hat. Zimmie saw herself misting into memory: his pregnant friend, his rebel girl. Of course she could manage without him. It was just that she didn't want to. The third truck that passed squealed onto the gravel. Chopper ran for it, waving once as he disappeared into the cab.

Son of a bitch, Zimmie murmured, how did I let myself get so dependent on a man, any man? I'm not the type to be dependent. And if I am, how come I let him slip away like that with his collapsible fishing pole in his knapsack? Sure, Chopper, do what you want, it might do you good to get away by yourself for a while, get out of this stinking town. That's not how to keep a man around. How to Keep a Man Around. Cling desperately. Claw on his hand. But I'd never make it without you honey; I'd just fall right apart.

You'se a buckin' kickin' stallion
I'll open the corral for you
I won't fence you in darlin'
If leaving's what you need to do

Zimmie glanced across the familiar Iowa fields. Each rippling hill had a white house and a red barn stuck on its side. She wanted to fall down, lie down on the grass beside the highway, but the straw was scratchy and the weeds shook like a row of fists in the dust blown up by passing cars. The changing patterns of sun and shade on the gravel made her look out at the open sky. She stretched her neck back, gazing up, the immense curve giving her a moment of relief from herself as she watched the wind push the clouds towards the horizon. She turned slowly away from the countryside, crossing back over the highway. She couldn't go home. She'd go downtown.

I'm an odd sort of woman
Rambling through this pregnancy
Trying to do best for my baby
Wondering: what is gonna happen to me

Isabel was sizzling tomato paste with sausage and chopped meat. She was beginning to feel the effects of the tranquilizer she swallowed an hour before when the din of three hungry children grew too loud. "How was your day?" she said to her husband as he banged in the door with a don't-ask expression on his face.

"I've had it with teaching," he announced, filling up the doorway to the kitchen with his long body. "I spent forty-five minutes giving what I thought was a passionate defense of Jacksonian democracy. When I was finished I asked if there were any questions and three hands shot up. 'Is this gonna be on the final?' "

Isabel smiled in sympathy. "Oh, we were like that too."

"No, we weren't," he said, glaring at her. "We were interested."

"Not in all classes," she said, her voice winding off as she saw his expression harden. He planted a chair between the refrigerator and the stove so Isabel had to squeeze past him to get the garlic, then squeeze back, bumping her hip against the sink.

"Izzy, there's something I have to tell you. I hope it doesn't upset you too much."

She added water to the pot, scraping the paste off the bottom with a wooden paddle. "You broke another thermos." Brian never laughed at her jokes—on principle, Isabel thought; it might encourage her to become a wise guy.

"I slept with another woman, Isabel." She shook oregano flakes over the pot, stirring them deep into the bubbling red sauce. "Did you hear me . . . ?"

"I heard you." She stopped stirring, watching his brown eyes, shaped like overturned bowls that concealed rather than revealed his thoughts.

"I decided I have to tell you about it. I've been feeling guilty for so long, I can't get it off my mind. It's hard because you're such a good person, I really feel like a louse."

"You got some mail today, something from the department," Isabel said, "I put it on—"

He was staring hard at the edge of chrome around the sink. "It was about two years ago. You were pregnant at the time. I was out riding on the Harley—the first Harley—and I saw this chick hitchhiking. She was kind of a mess, with curly black hair frizzing all over. As I was passing, her skirt flapped up and I saw she wasn't wearing any panties." The tomato sauce boiled over, spitting onto the stove. "So I stopped for her; I just couldn't resist. I asked her where she was going and she said, 'For a ride, anywhere.' When she got on the bike she put her hands right around my crotch"—Isabel leaned over, flipping off the heat under the sauce, which was cascading over the sides of the pot—"and rubbed her tits into my back. I couldn't keep the bike balanced. We did it twice, in the ditch. She was crazy. As soon as it was over her eyes glazed and she started hitchhiking again. Wouldn't even let me take her for a hamburger. I turned the bike around and came home to you. I remember you were crocheting a blanket and reading to Janey at the same time."

Isabel burned her finger trying to sponge up the mess on the stove. There was crying coming from the living room, like a siren leaving town. She didn't quite believe the story. Brian, her prudish husband who leaped under the covers the moment he had his clothes off? In the ditch in broad daylight? "What was her name?" Isabel asked.

"Judy." He looked up at her, his eyes skipping from her face to over her shoulder to his shoes.

"I'm glad you didn't tell me about it when I was pregnant," she said finally.

Brian jumped up, knocking over his chair. "Is that all you can say? After I've been feeling guilty for two years? I guess it's o.k., then. I can just ball whoever I want to."

Isabel was reminded of a burning tower at the circus with clowns running through the smoke fighting the simulated flames. The emergency seemed bogus; but she was not a spectator, she was expected to heed his noisy alarm. What did he want her to do? She felt a hot sensation in her bowels. She believed the story. Her hand trembled as she grabbed her pocketbook, tripped over Marty, banged her ankle against his truck, reached the front door, hauled it open, and stumbled out into the street. She sprinted for three blocks until she reached the bridge over the railroad tracks, where she stopped to put on her sunglasses. Usually when she reached the overpass she stopped to admire the wildflowers growing between the tracks and talk herself into going back home. The blood beating in her head seemed to push the tears from

her eyes in a rhythmical rain. She leaned against the railing
a few moments, then began to walk quickly down past the
hospital complex, under the campus elms, past the girls'
dormitories into the suppertime emptiness of the downtown
area.

The Iowa sunset was splashed orange over the low gray
town. Everyone said the gnats were terrible this spring. They
hovered around Zimmie's eyes. Chopper said she should kill
some of them instead of just waving them away: at least
eliminate the ones that attack you personally. Chopper said,
Chopper said. How was she going to handle the Mainliner
crowd tonight? "Hi, Zimmie, where's Chopper?" When she
tells them, will they study her for signs of fear and misery,
recalling her boasts about their free relationship?

The supermarket manager who caught Zimmie with a
sirloin steak under her dress last winter is crossing the street
towards her. She pulls her hair over her eyes, scuffing her
sandals, grinding her teeth like the swamp rat she still is in
her gut, though the time for that is past. The manager is rolling his weary eyeballs along the sidewalk; he doesn't recognize her.

> I'm an odd sort of woman
> Don't wonder at me—
> Just walk by

There's only an occasional car on the street. The sidewalks
loom wide and white under the sandals slapping at her heels.
A man hurries out the side door of the drugstore with a
white package. Maybe it's early enough for Zimmie to get a
pizza and beer at the bar without running into any of their
regular friends. Maybe she'll just eat and go home early and
get stoned on the two ounces of grass Chopper tucked under
his mattress.

Isabel Schneider is leaning against the drugstore window with tears dripping out from under her sunglasses. Zimmie nods and starts to walk by, then turns back, noticing the tissue clutched tightly in Isabel's fist. "Hi, Isabel. I didn't recognize you."

"Oh hello, Zimmie. I haven't seen you in so long." She is staring at Zimmie's stomach bulging like an oversized lemon under her yellow smock. Whose baby is it? Isabel wonders, she isn't married, is she? The poor kid, no one mentioned she was pregnant. "I wondered why you weren't volunteering at the daycare anymore," Isabel says, her eyes suddenly dry and burning. "When are you due?"

"July ninth," Zimmie says. "Soon."

"Whose—what doctor are you using?"

"Uh, the clinic. I was there yesterday and they let me listen to the baby's heartbeat on this machine. It really boomed!" Just saying this releases a steam of pressure from Zimmie's heart: someone to talk to about it.

"I used Dr. Greenwalk," Isabel says.

"Oh yeah? I heard he encourages everyone to have four, five kids."

"I guess he does. People with such high intelligence and fine character as Brian and I should consider it our duty, and all that. I really ate up that advice. I just loved being pregnant. Don't you feel special?" Zimmie nods doubtfully, leaning against the glass next to Isabel, who flounders, "I guess it depends on the situation. Are you . . . well, whose baby is it?"

Zimmie folds her arms across her stomach. "Uh, mine. You might say this is an IUD baby who didn't show up on the rabbit test until he was three months old." Isabel looks concerned, wrinkling between the eyebrows over the brown rims of her sunglasses. "I'm glad I'm having him, though. I'm going to raise the most far-out kid—he's going to be the revolution. I'm going to call him Che Guevara."

Dark clouds are moving in, blotting up the orange sunset. Isabel tosses her tissue into the gutter. "How do you find it over at the clinic?"

"Oh, the doctors are pretty straight and all. This one doctor won't even see me anymore. He asked me if I took any drugs, so I said, 'Uh, THC.' 'What?' 'Uh, cannabis, you know.' I figured I had to use big words with doctors. He looked blank, screwing around with his fountain pen, so I said, 'Uh, marijuana.' 'Oh.' He nods his head gravely. 'How often have you . . . done it?' 'Done what?' 'Used the drug?' 'Oh, uhhhh.' 'Ten times?' 'Uh.' 'Fifteen times?' 'Uh.' "

Isabel is laughing, watching Zimmie's face change from stern to stupid as she recounts the dialogue.

" 'Don't you know how many times you've done it?' 'Uh.' 'More or less than one hundred times?' 'Uh.' 'More than one hundred times?' 'Uh, yeah.' Then he leaps up and runs out of the office. I was freaking out, wondering if smoking pot would disqualify me for clinic care or something, thinking maybe I should have the baby at Scarecrow's commune squatting in their Queen Cleopatra chair, dropping the baby through the hole in the seat into Scarecrow's dirty fingernails. Then this young doctor with a thick black beard comes into the office. 'I'm Dr. Crinose,' he says. 'I understand you smoke grass.'

"I just ignored that and started telling him how I want a natural childbirth by the Lamaze method, you know, breathing and stuff without any drugs. You did it that way, didn't you? I told him I wanted to experience the whole thing, so when my kid asks me about it someday I can tell him I was there. Crinose is nodding at me; he seems to get shorter and shorter as he smiles. 'In other words, you want a stoned pregnancy but a natural childbirth.' I just grinned back at him and said, 'Don't you just love contradictions?' Now he's about the only doctor at the clinic who'll have anything to do with me. It's like having a private doctor."

Zimmie peers through Isabel's sunglasses, trying to see

how she's taking all this. It's almost dark near the ground now, but there's still a blue-sky circle above the town. "Say, Isabel, I just moved into a new house on Warbler Street. Do you want to walk uptown and see it?" Zimmie wonders why Isabel is out wandering during the dinner hour instead of home cooking it up for her husband and kids.

"Yeah, why not?" Isabel straightens up off the side of the building, forcing herself to walk slowly to fall in with Zimmie's ambling pace, thinking about how her own legs ached during pregnancy, how she felt like the center of the world, radiating circles of peace and calm. She feels more comfortable with Zimmie now that her body is bursting with life than she did last year when they'd met across a crying child at the daycare center, when just the sight of Zimmie's breasts bouncing freely under a T-shirt and her easy collapsing sprawls made Isabel clutch tightly at Brian's arm.

They reach Zimmie's house, which is way at the end of the block, practically out of town; you can hear the highway thunder from the porch. Zimmie is so glad to have someone to show her new house to. It's the nicest she's ever had. A porch with a creaky swing, big dusty rooms with cartons in the corners, a kitchen with a window over the sink and a good green view of a yardful of trees. "Can I call my husband?" Isabel asks.

"The phone's not in yet. Let him suffer awhile, will you?" Zimmie remembers Brian Schneider, tall and skinny, brown eyes filled with supreme boredom at all the dull people surrounding him, steering his wife through crowds with a hand on her elbow. Surely he can stand a little suffering.

Isabel sits down in the bare kitchen. She notices that Zimmie doesn't have a paper-towel–wax-paper–foil dispenser, or a spice rack full of tiny jars, or a rack of knives, or a display of antique spoons. There is nothing to suggest the fulfilled homemaker, an image Isabel has spent busy hours in hardware stores shopping for with anniversary checks from

Brian's mother. And a lot of good it's done her. Zimmie bends in front of the refrigerator to get some beer. Isabel notices the refrigerator is almost empty: the shelf grids and white sides loom. She feels tears forming again, tries to suck them back into her nose and mouth. Bad enough she charged out of the house. Did she have to forget her tranquilizers? Couldn't she have charged past the medicine cabinet first? The tears are splashing in her lap.

"Tell me the whole rotten story," Zimmie says.

"Ohhhhh."

Zimmie tries to wait while Isabel struggles down her tears. But waiting is hard for Zimmie. She prowls around the kitchen, her arms curling. Finally, leaning her arms on the sill, she sings softly to her reflection in the window glass:

> Tell me the whole rotten story
> Down to the last detail
> I want to know all about it
> Every laugh and crying wail

"It's about your husband."

"The kids are great, my job is great—I've got the largest enrollment ever in my swimming classes—all the appliances in the house are working—"

"Count those blessings."

"—the garden is growing, I don't have a cold or my period—"

"So it must be your husband." Zimmie feels like she's yanking a fish from the pond. She'd love to see Isabel steam off a little pressure. Isabel's tears are controlled now, but her body is struggling with emotion. She sits on her legs for a moment, then stretches them out, pointing toe, heel, then crosses her legs until her white shorts cut at her crotch and she rises slightly to pull her shorts down. Zimmie moves slowly to the table, sitting across from Isabel. "Oh tell me about it."

I gotta know all about it
Down to the last detail

Isabel's sunglasses are off now. She has teacup-blue eyes which fixate on one spot and forget to move. She has the kind of long! blond! hair which curves up at the ends. Zimmie pictures a haymaking machine mowing over Isabel's head, packing her hair into neat square bundles on top of a bald skull. She'd still be pretty.

"When you're married," Isabel starts slowly, "everything becomes a secret between you and your husband." She tells the story in a clipped voice, stressing that everything had been going along fine, just fine, until Brian slammed in the door and gave his impromptu confession. And even after she heard the whole story, hands around crotch and all, she still didn't react much until he prodded deeper, demanding some sort of reaction that Isabel had lost the script for. She tells Zimmie word for word what Brian had spoken, her brain his perfect stenographer. "And all those years I was certain Brian would *never* make love to anyone else. He's too shy, too much of a puritan. If I try to seduce him he hates it. He just wants me to lie there in a white nightgown and move as little as possible. He grew up with four sisters and a mother who made him get dressed in the bathroom. Now I feel that I haven't known him at all."

Isabel gave the story to Zimmie whole, wrapped and wound with a ribbon, and now she watches Zimmie tearing it open, examining the flaws, guessing the price. "So you just ran out of the house crying? I wonder what made him decide to tell you." Zimmie paces heavily around the kitchen, leaning on the window sill, the sink, the counter. I don't like your husband, she wants to say, you're so much nicer than he is. They're drinking beer out of the cans. Maybe Zimmie should wash out some glasses, as Isabel would certainly do if it were her house, but she doesn't want to. She's thinking about what she'd like to do to Brian Schneider. Set fire to his mustache. Kick his shins. Ball him in the ditch. Lucky star that Zimmie is not, never will be, never wants to be, married. She feels she should say something to Isabel about the incident, but looking at her, maybe she doesn't need to. A few flecks of sunshine are rising in her teacup eyes. When Isabel smiles her freckles pop out.

The baby is kicking in a blues pattern. "Feel this, Isabel."

Her hand is cool on Zimmie's belly. "Let me see." Zimmie lifts her dress; she isn't wearing panties. There are blue stretch lines on her cauliflower stomach. "The happiest times of my life were when I was pregnant," Isabel murmurs.

Zimmie and Isabel hold hands as they talk, their arms forming a hoop around the protruding stranger. "Yesterday when I was taking a bath," Zimmie says, "my stomach hurt so I pushed it out about three inches. Then I couldn't pull it back. It grew right before my eyes."

Isabel feels a chunk of herself wobbling around the hoop to her friend. "This is fantastic. I never thought I'd get any relief tonight."

"How old are you, Isabel?"

"Twenty-nine. You?"

"Twenty-one." Just saying it makes Zimmie's throat stick. Twenty-one is past the prime for a revolutionary, she believes. Especially twenty-one in 1972. A disaster. As someone who wants to blow things up, assassinate political enemies, topple the whole social structure and then rebuild it into a workable order, she feels the aching pressure of time. She slips her hands away from Isabel and broods out the window on this. When she turns back on the room, Isabel's teacup eyes are pouring out big drops of water again.

"You know, I think crying is counter-revolutionary."

Hard laughter brings me power
There ain't no man can make me cry—

I believe in revolutionary laughter. Listen, Iz, I grew up in the sixties. I didn't think the riots were just going to peter out. I thought we had all the time in the world to practice playing revolution, stalking around like swamp rats, ripping off the ruling class, getting strong and stoned and ready. Meanwhile the power structure was over-eating, bloating itself on dead students and burned Vietnamese babies and gagging on the rotten taste of its own napalm. Then just at the right moment all the underground people would arise with a mighty yell and punch the ruling class in the stomach. Kaploom! Revolution in the streets.

"I never reckoned on 1972. I didn't think everyone would spread thin and turn inward and try to work the damn system. What happened to the revolution? I think about that all the time. It's hiding in the hearts of the people. I think it's revolutionary to laugh. You know, like me being pregnant despite all this modern technology and very little sex. I want to raise this kid to be an absolute freak and his own person. We'll just make up our lives as we go along instead of stuffing them into a mold. I'll tell the kid all about 1968 and 1969— great years for revolution. I wish I could figure out where all that energy went. Do you want to hear my theory?"

Isabel nods, quite distracted from Judy in the Ditch for the moment. "I guess you mean all the riots and demonstrations. I was into that too, then; I even got arrested right here in Candle City for blockading the Marine recruiters inside the Student Union."

"Did they drag you by your long blond hair?"

"Oh no. I was with the dignified liberal contingent. We walked all the way to jail."

"Well, this is my theory." Zimmie opens a kitchen drawer and pulls out a bunch of wrinkled clippings from *Natural History*. "Here we go: *The prospect of looking so far back in time excites astronomers as much as anything else about quasars.*"

"Quasars? I thought I was going to get political theory. Wait until I wash my face; my cheeks are stiff."

Zimmie waits impatiently; the baby pushes up against her rib cage, her thoughts whirl with the excitement she and Chopper had generated in the yard every night, gazing at the stars, sharing cosmic theories. Would anyone else understand about black holes? If not, if it was just a private rap, then what was it worth? Oh, she liked Isabel. It seemed impossible that Zimmie Roland Alp could like a girl with long blond hair and beautiful eyes and nothing at all wrong with her looks. Well, Isabel was flat-chested, Zimmie thought with a certain relief. If she had been big-busted as well it would have been too much to bear. Not that Zimmie was so crazy about her own large breasts, resting like fat cats curled on her stomach. But she had found that men appreciate them, and when you have ratty brown hair and a chipmunk face, it was a comfort to know there was something about you that men appreciated.

I'm an odd sort of woman
Alone alone and I know why
I never wear make-up, honey
I never giggle, squeal, or sigh

"You're always singing!" Isabel said.

"I'm going to be a great folksinger someday," Zimmie says, "as soon as I finish revolutionizing American society. Now, are you ready for cosmology?"

"I guess so."

Zimmie finds if she looks very steadily into Isabel's eyes she can forget about how pretty she is and see the flickering interest. "Well, cosmology is the basis for your whole outlook on life, don't you think? Like have you ever thought about where astrology freaks are at? I don't mean the ones who say 'What's your sign?' at parties as if they could get some instant advance information about whether you'll be compatible in bed and not deal with the real questions like 'What position do you like best?' 'Do you like to be beat or do the beating?' 'Do you like it light and sensual or rough and bruising?' "

"Delightful questions," said Isabel, stretching her feet onto the empty kitchen chair. "Let's remember to talk about that sometime."

Zimmie clutches her clippings. "O.k., so I mean the people who use astrology as a cosmic view. Like if you say to my friend, 'Fred, you're such a good sculptor, why do you sit around stoned all day instead of working at it?' he'll say, 'Oh, my Jupiter is aligned to my right ball today and I can't get a thing done. You know I'm a triple Scorpio, so don't criticize me, please; just love me the way I am or I get very dangerous.' Are you following this?"

"Well, a little," Isabel said when she stops laughing. "You mean astrology people are fatalistic."

"Exactly!" Zimmie sits down across the table and smiles like an apple. "Astrology is counter-revolutionary. You can't make a revolution unless you believe you can. Those people never even try to change themselves in a conscious way."

Do I? thinks Isabel. I usually try to change Brian, or the kids.

"Fred keeps talking about the big famine that's coming in 1982. Maybe he's laying in a little grain. O.k., so we're not astrology freaks, but what else is there? In science—astronomy—incredible things are being discovered. Like black holes: *Hot young massive stars* . . . I can identify with that. Don't I look like a hot young massive star? *Hot young massive stars tend to blow up in SUPER NOVA explosions. For a few weeks the star radiates the energy of a whole galaxy. Then, what is left, if anything, collapses in on itself to produce a superdense neutron star. Or, a BLACK HOLE.*"

There's no reaction from Isabel and Zimmie feels frustrated at understanding this astronomy stuff only a little. It seems so important. "That was 1968," Zimmie says, "a hot young massive revolution that blew up and by 1969 radiated the fantastic energy of a whole turned-on generation scream-ing 'This society is shit,' and then, what was left, if any-thing, collapsed in on itself—that's happening right now—and by the eighties we'll all be in a black hole."

Isabel sighs, shifting positions. "You reached the same con-clusion as Fred the astrologer. I have kids, Zimmie. You'll have one soon. Pessimism and motherhood are a lousy com-bination."

That sets Zimmie back. She slumps in the hard-backed kitchen chair, belly, breasts, head, like a pyramid of melons.

After a silence she raises her chin and reads from another clipping: "*Ryan goes on to suggest that every galaxy with a mass of 10 million suns or more may have a* . . . O.k., Iz, forget what I said before. This stuff really can't be applied directly to the political situation. It's just interesting as cos-mology. *There is some physical evidence pointing to a black hole at the center of our galaxy.* Isn't that incredible? Like Alice falling down the rabbit hole or something. *The prob-lem with black holes*—I love this part!—*is that there's no way to see them or hear them. You couldn't see one if it was right in front of you. A black hole is a rapidly*

> *rotating*
> *collapsed*
> *object*

detectable only by the attraction it exerts on other matter and the resulting radiation. Now I see what was wrong with what I said before," Zimmie adds. "The black hole isn't the end of anything. It's just a stage: *Suppose, as many do, that the universe is oscillating* . . . whaaaaaang—*According to one theory there is a big bang* . . . kaboom—*The universe expands, then gradually slows down, then compresses into one glowing mass, which explodes in another big bang* . . .

kaboom—You dig it? There's a series of these reactions over millions and killions of years. Hot! Young! Massive! Stars! Kaboom! Black holes spinning faster and getting hotter and hotter! Kaboom! Stars again. O.k.?"

Zimmie exclaimed herself out of her seat, hopping around the kitchen. "Now get this; this is the science-fiction part. *No one is sure that the physical laws we know remain the same in each succeeding universe.* In each succeeding universe. I love that phrase. Evolution on the highest scale. *In each succeeding universe time may flow in the opposite direction.* Now isn't that incredible? Not far from the thought of riding a time machine back into history to stand over Lenin's shoulder to find out how he kept it together all those years in exile waiting for the historically ripe moment. *Thus, the radiation we see today is the starlight of a universe yet to be unscrambled and made isotopic by a big bang.* I looked up *isotopic* and it means 'changed beyond belief.' The starlight of a universe yet to be unscrambled and made isotopic by a big belief. There, well, what do you think of it?"

Isabel laughs. "When I go home I'll tell Brian we talked about cooking and baby clothes."

Isn't it amazing how marriage makes a person keep the lid on? Zimmie thought.

"It seems very abstract, Zimmie. What meaning does it have for you?"

"If the outer crust of reality . . . the stars . . . uh, change and move in and out of existence, then everything we are is part of that bigger motion. It's just a matter of finding a philosophy, I guess. It doesn't matter whether you study evolution of snails, or capitalism. I happen to get off on keeping track of how the universe is changing. I always feel like I want to understand everything."

Isabel shakes her head. "I usually feel I'm better off not knowing."

Zimmie's face is wet with sweat. She pulls down the elastic neck of her dress to let some air in. Isabel is still perched on the corner of her kitchen chair.

"You know what Chopper says about me," said Zimmie, pushing the damp hair off her forehead. " 'Zimmie likes any slogan with the word NOW in it.' I figured pregnancy was a good time to study patience. What's slower than the evolution of the universe? And yet, though it takes killions of years to build up the energy for change, when it does happen it happens suddenly—kaboom!" Zimmie is exhausted from the conversation. Her stomach is heavy. She feels like pushing the huge medicine ball to Isabel.

Standing up slowly, Zimmie opens the back door and beckons Isabel into the brown June night. The elm trees shiver darkly around the yard. Zimmie stretches flat on the grass, lifting her stomach off her groin with her fingers. It's late, Isabel thinks. Brian would be wondering about her. Many times she'd run out of the house crying, but she never found anywhere to go before. Home to Brian . . . what would happen? A rehash of Judy in the Ditch. A crust of tomato sauce on the stove. Kids: up? sleeping? Toys all over the living room. The hot steamy thoughts carried blurred images of the black curly hair on Brian's chest. Beneath the steam was the ice-cold feeling: who cares what he does? She was so tired of worrying about how Brian would think, how he would react, how she could maneuver the life of the family so it didn't interfere with his work, his football games. She was tired of him. The ice touched her heart, pinching. No, she tells herself firmly, I'm not tired of him. In fact, his screwing in the ditch might stir a new interest. I'm lying to myself, she thinks, tears stinging the corners of her eyes, why did I forget my Valiums? Little yellows. Why don't I remember to buy myself a pill box and keep them always in my purse? I'd feel so much better now if I'd taken a Valium before I left. After a while she hears Zimmie singing, her voice mingling with the night sounds of crickets and leaves in the soft wind.

Oh Zimmie knows the jailhouse well
So modern and humane
The matron has a fruit-gum smile
The sheriff knows her name

Nineteen-hundred and sixty-eight
A long explosive year—
Revolution didn't hesitate
There was no such thing as fear

Zimmie rolls over onto her side so she can rise off the lawn.

"I should call Brian," Isabel said in a wet voice.

"I'll be getting my phone tomorrow if you want to wait till then," Zimmie said. "I went to the phone company to give my deposit yesterday. It was a riot." She slips her arm around Isabel, leading her back to the kitchen. "The woman says, 'In whose name do you want the phone?' ' Z. R. Alp,' I say. 'Is that Mr. Z. R. Alp?' 'Uh, no.' 'Mrs. Z. R. Alp?' 'No, I'm not married.' She actually leaned over the counter to get a good look at my belly. 'What's your occupation, Miss?' Occupation? Hummmm? That stuck me. Why do they ask such hard questions? Let's see, unemployed folksinger? Welfare-mother-to-be? Occupation. 'Oh, I know. I'm a housewife.' 'What?' she says. 'How can you be a housewife if you're not married?' 'Uh, it's much easier, actually. No man to pick up after. I'm married to the house.' "

2

Yes we called ourselves the swamp rats
And we longed to make t.v.
Fire bombs, slogans, and arson
Were our home-town specialty

"How am I going to get home? I can't call Brian. The kids are sleeping; I wouldn't want him to leave them."

"Walk."

"What? It's dark. Do you know there've been eleven rapes in Candle City this year?"

"Well, wait till it's light then. Just a few more hours."

"I could call a cab."

"You could. You don't really want to leave."

"No. It serves him right, don't you think?"

"I'm sure he went to sleep by now."

"But I never do things like this. I'm the good wife. I've never stayed out all night."

Zimmie walks towards the bathroom. "Well, think it out. Let's not spend all night talking about whether you're going or staying."

"Pregnant women can't stay up all night."

"Oh, why not?" Zimmie called through the bathroom door. "I'll sleep all day tomorrow."

Isabel curls up on the scratchy sofa. If she went home she could take a tranquilizer. Being up on pills was like lying on a hammock, gently rocking. It wasn't so comfortable at first. She had to force her body to slump, steady, relax. The rough cord cut into her back. It was hard to adjust to the new curve of mind, to keep her body balanced. She couldn't exert her body in any way. If she stuck a leg over the side to stop the almost imperceptible swaying, she would tip the hammock.

But if she kept her legs straight, her arms at her side, her head back, her breathing light and regular, oh, there was nothing more comfortable than that hammock. Things became very easy. She swayed in the warm breeze, avoiding sudden thoughts and dangerous inspirations that would upset the balance. She kept her mind on details. Things became very easy.

Daydreaming about taking a Valium was not the same thing as taking one. Isabel felt the dry ice smoldering in her chest. Though she's forced her body to relax on the rough upholstery, she feels uneasy. I'll call a cab, she decides, springing up on her long swimmer's legs. But there's no phone. "How can I call a cab if there's no telephone?" she wails as Zimmie comes out of the bathroom.

"Do you miss Brian that much?"

"I forgot my pills," Isabel said. "I'm supposed to take three tranquilizers a day."

"Yeah? For how long?"

"Oh, as long as the marriage lasts, I guess."

"That's a lot of shit!" Zimmie said. "Don't take 'em!"

"Oh, they really work," said Isabel. "I wouldn't be crying so much if I took them. I don't bitch as much to Brian. I don't worry about things. It is hard on the children, though. They always want me to *be there*, kind of, and I'm just drifting in the general vicinity."

Zimmie falls into the heavy leather rocking chair, trying to put her finger on what's wrong with what Isabel is saying. Who wants to be tranquil; is that a natural desire? Zimmie is addicted to excitement, turmoil. "Well, Chopper told me this story about a professional basketball player he knows and idolizes. He went up to the house to see him and found the guy's wife really spaced out. She was waltzing around by herself, laughing like champagne. It seems the team doctor prescribes tranquilizers to all the basketball wives so they won't sleep around while the men are on the road. Of course the husbands sleep around. Then this doc told the wives to keep taking the pills when their husbands came home so they'll have fewer arguments. Good for the game."

"Good for the marriage," Isabel says staunchly. Zimmie begins humming blues bars. The words slip out as if she were remembering them from somewhere instead of making them up on the spot.

> I got the tranquilizer blues
> The little yellow tranquilizer blues
>
> I don't feel nothing
> That I don't want to feel
> I'm not always with it
> And I'm not always real
>
> But at least I'm not crying
> Or showing too much will
> I'm sticking to that man of mine
> And that little yellow pill
>
> I've got the tranquilizer blues
> The three-a-day blues. . . .

"How do you do that?" Isabel demanded.

"Chopper says I was born singing the blues." Zimmie felt her spirit expanding out of her body, filling the room with mythic grandeur.

"Who's this Chopper?" Isabel asked. Her irritation was subsiding again. There was something about just being near a pregnant woman which relaxed her. If she presses closer to Zimmie's warm roundness, she can ignore the persistent image of a girl and a man tumbling over a motorcycle into a ditch.

Explain Chopper to Isabel: there was a task. Could Isabel understand? Did Zimmie understand? "Well, dearie, Chopper is my main love, my revolutionary hero, my roommate when he's in town, which he isn't right now."

"Is it his baby?"

"No. No way. I think he'll be into the kid when it comes, though. Unless he finds some really neat girl in Aspen, Colorado, who has the sense to marry him up and chain him to a job instead of letting him wander all over the place like I do. I have this nightmare about a rich girl in Aspen with long shiny hair like yours . . . but I can't let myself get too morbid. Chopper is . . ." She stands up slowly and pushes open the door to Chopper's room, waving Isabel along.

Isabel studies the blue wall covered with pictures unevenly cut from sports magazines of batters swinging, pitchers rearing up on the mound, runners sliding, umpires, red in the face, screaming over heaps of fighting St. Louis Cardinals. There's sports debris on the floor: a hardball, a softball, a brand new football, a worn football coming unstrung, a basketball, a glove, newly oiled and tied around a hardball to improve the pocket, several bats, including a junior-size one, his first, knee guards, T-shirts with numbers on them.

"Wow, a jock," Isabel says.

"Uh, sort of."

Isabel twirls the basketball on her long fingers and shoots at the poster of Lenin over Chopper's bed. "Is he on a university team?"

"Well, he was on a scholarship before . . . It's a long story. He was the star of his high school team and his father worked two jobs so Chopper could have a car and wouldn't take an after-school job like the other working-class kids. He wanted Chopper to, you know, be a star and get ahead. All the other kids on the team were from rich families, lawyers and accountants and stuff, because the poor kids worked after school setting up pins in bowling alleys. Then one day a bunch of these general students who called themselves the Mangy Mobsters challenged the Flashers to a basketball game and beat the pants off them. Chopper freaked out: says it changed his whole life. I mean his team got to practice in the gym every day, good food, lots of sleep, coaching, while the Mobsters never worked out except in the playground after dark. Chopper thought he was real superior to those guys— but how could he be superior to someone who played better basketball? Anyway he made friends with the Mobsters and played ball with them whenever they were free and became a revolutionary. Does that explain anything? It's hard to explain a person like Chopper—he's complex."

"Is he in love with you?" Isabel asks.

Zimmie laughs. Right down to it, huh.

"Will he be with you when you give birth?"

"You're more interested in me than hearing about him, huh?"

"Well, you're pregnant . . . I don't know . . . he's. . . All right, tell me some more about your relationship."

Zimmie sits down on the crumpled bed. "Our Relationship. We discuss it a lot, all the time in fact. We just try to stay as free as possible. Like I never go to his games, even though he likes winning best when there's a girl in the stands to see it. We don't do things just for each other."

Isabel is crouching on the floor, picking through a tangle of cables and connectors, trying to absorb Zimmie's words as the dry ice burns her chest. Everything she does is for Brian or the children. Everything? Sometimes she buys rye crackers with caraway seeds that only she likes. "What is this stuff?"

"Video-tape business. He's a media major; I've been in some t.v. programs he filmed." She reaches above the bed for the light, tries to jump up, forgetting her condition; Isabel reaches out to help her, leading the way out of the room.

Zimmie pulls the warped door hard to close it. "I love to talk to him and fuck with him, but I can't stand living with his things. They make me feel weird. And he's a worse mess than I am."

They settle down in the living room, Isabel stretched on the couch, Zimmie lying on the worn Oriental rug slowly raising and lowering one leg at a time.

"Will he be with you when you give birth?" Isabel asks again.

Zimmie points her toes way out as she lowers her leg. "I don't think I'd want him there. I'd rather be alone: mighty mother Alp and the forces of the universe."

Isabel doesn't laugh at that. "I wonder if they'd let a woman come in? My doctor acted like he was granting a big favor to let *the husband* be present. I'd love to see a birth, to be the one standing up, helping."

Zimmie raises her other leg, poised on a decision. Should she ask Isabel to be with her? Will she still know her in two weeks? What if Isabel forgets about Judy in the Ditch and makes it up with Brian? Will he ever let her out again? She's used to thinking of this pregnancy as her own solitary walk. Z. R. Alp, champion mother, never a trace of morning sickness, dizzy-spelling, weird craving, or complaining. "I can do it alone," she said.

"For a revolutionary, you sure don't put any stock in collective effort."

"I only hope," Zimmie said, "that giving birth is as exciting as the night the metal bit the stars in Muskmelon, Iowa." She rises off the floor and falls into the rocking chair, pushing off into a song:

Zimmie was leader of the rats
That's an undisputed claim
Murray made bombs and got the dope
And Mr. Doom sat around hating the motherfuckers

"I guess I'll have to tell you this story myself. Usually I do it when Chopper's around and he gives the introduction. He stands up and grabs a magazine: 'As one US State Department official said in the October 7, 1968, issue of *Newsweek*, 'These kids are all trying to tell us something—and we had better well figure out what it is.' Then I poke him with my elbow and say, 'I can tell this story by myself, Lightning Mouth, I don't need any help from you.'"

Isabel snuggles down on the sofa, pulling the crocheted afghan she found on the floor over her. She tries to pretend she feels the soft swaying of the Valium within her.

"I was seventeen, see. Every day I lay on the rug in front of the television watching young people screaming at old people on the five thirty news." Zimmie rocks her chair furiously, tossing her face forwards and back as she talks. "There were kids screaming at cops, throwing rocks at cops, running from cops, getting beat by cops and trampled by horses. I was coming into a revolutionary heat. My dungarees hitched up around my crotch, my legs aching for action, as I hung onto the faces of bearded boys and stringy-haired girls reciting nonnegotiable demands into duly elected gray faces.

"I had some buddies. There was Mr. Doom, a farm boy they sent over to Vietnam who brought back the first good hash I ever smoked and a deeply disturbed brain. He was sure there was a GI rebellion coming any day. With no provocation he'd leap up tall and skinny and let the bullets rat-a-tat-tat down his jerking arm, while the other arm whirled above his head like a helicopter blade and his eyes bulged down at the gooks running, looking back over their shoulders: 'I was their doooooommmmmm.' And the poor guy spent all day working on his dad's farm listening to 'All this will be yours someday, son. You earned it. You fought to keep it free.' All that mud, corn, and fence. At night he took three showers to get the pig smell off him and came to town with his hair slicked wet." Zimmie smiles at Isabel, appreciating the blue light of curiosity in her eyes. "Well, it was

Zimmie, Murray, and Mr. Doom
Hanging stoned in Murray's room
When Murray says so casually
'Know what I learned in chemistry?'

"Murray built the first bomb in a Coke bottle. Mr. Doom
ran it down to the service road in a brown paper bag. I took
it the rest of the way, wearing dark clothes and boy's sneakers, my mouth tasting of maple syrup. There was a cold Iowa
wind cleaning my nostrils and I kept thinking I smelled
clover as I ran. I opened the door of this long blue shiny
gleaming clean police car, tucked the bomb into the driver's
seat, flinging my hair off my neck so I could breathe. There
was that smell of clover. I touched the shiny blue steering
wheel, the crotchety vinyl seat. I couldn't read the mileage
in the dark. I closed the car door quietly, paced back five
hundred feet, and chalked big letters on the black parking-lot
floor: BRING THE WAR HOME.

"Then I ran back to the service road, kneeling in the
dry grass and clover. I waited. Oh, no, it'll never go off and
I'll get caught anyway! Oh, these pure cold moments of
political virginhood as I step into revolutionary beingness.
Oh, it'll go off and it won't mean a damn! Next time the
White House. No moon tonight. I tied my sneaker laces
tighter. The stars were dim and far.

KABLOOM!

The car bit the stars. It heaved way up and held an instant
with the hood rising, the doors flying open, a big yellow scrib-
ble of light in the sky. Then crashing glass and crunching
metal. The upholstery bounced. The tires groaned. The car
hit the parking lot. It was better than television. I felt fantastic: older, braver, incredibly excited. I heard Sheriff Mantelface yell as he came running out of the diner and took off."

Zimmie is stretched back on the rocker, her hands resting
on her belly mound, her eyes half-closed in memory.

We're gonna bring the war home
We're gonna bring the war home
Right here to Muskmelon, Iowa
We're gonna bring the war home

"You just made the whole thing up," Isabel said. "Is this some kind of official entertainment?"

Zimmie sat up. "Every word of it, the truth."

"You must have got caught."

"Oh yes. It took 'em three months, though. My parents fucked me over. Just the sight of the sheriff at the front door and my father knew I'd done it. I was always a rotten kid. They strapped me to a lie detector, questioning me for three days. I lied about everything, thinking I'd confuse the machine. The table was designed for a man. I'm just over five feet, so my arm ached from being strapped up so high. They brought my father in, finally. He was crying: 'Tell them the truth, Zimmie, it's the best thing, listen to your father. I'll get you off if you just tell the truth.' He had his arm around the sheriff's shoulder. I finally confessed, but I claimed I built the bomb myself and they never budged me from that position. They caught Mr. Doom, but neither of us ratted on Murray, who was back at the State University by this time and never suspected. Last I heard he was building munitions for the Weathermen. They fined us each three thousand dollars. My father had to get a loan for it, which he's still paying off. I was disappointed that the people in town hated us so much for it, even the kids. Last time I saw Mr. Doom he was still slopping pigs on his father's farm."

Oh Zimmie knows the jailhouse well
So modern and humane
The matron has a fruit-gum smile
And the sheriff knows her name

Isabel was still uncertain that the story was true. Was there any act in her own life that willful? It was getting very late. Her eyes were tired from the hour, from the crying. When Zimmie told the part about crouching in the ditch, Isabel saw a motorcycle next to her; she heard a couple screaming in wild passion. Somewhere she had heard about Zimmie getting arrested for shoplifting. And busted at a concert for pot. But this? Zimmie had disappeared into the kitchen. Isabel pushed the curtain aside. The street lamps seemed short against the darkness. The street was empty. We're probably the only people in town up at this hour, Isabel thought with disdain; if this was New York, oh, if this was New York. . . .

Now that Zimmie was out of the room Isabel scarcely believed in her. The large living room, practically empty of furniture, with its heavy, scratchy drapes and sofa and faded rug, seemed an apt prison for Isabel, Brian, Judy, and the motorcycle. From the kitchen she heard cupboards slamming, the refrigerator door squealing on its hinges. I've just spent an entire evening with a woman I hardly know, Isabel thought. I should have been home working it out with Brian, taking a tranquilizer, getting some sleep. Tomorrow . . . Oh, I won't think about that yet. Zimmie was so entertaining. Rather like the first few days she spent with Brian, eleven years before, when he wooed her away from her previous boyfriend (a champion swimmer) with exciting stories of his trip to New Orleans and getting ejected from the galleries in Congress for insisting on reading under the No Reading signs: "I don't make the rules around here," the guard said, to which Brian shouted, "I don't make the rules around here either, I break them!" In those days he spun beautiful dreams about staking out a claim in Alaska "to try to understand America. I'm obsessed with this country and its beautiful dream. I want to merge with it." He'd settled for graduate school in American Studies. Ach, maybe Zimmie wouldn't seem so exciting tomorrow. By then they'd be back to the humdrum questions: are you free next Tuesday afternoon? will you mind my kids while I run to the gynecologist? do you need some baby clothes? nursing bras? keep your hands off my husband! can you come to supper on the tenth? do you want a cutting from my wax begonia?

Zimmie was singing in the kitchen. Isabel opens the door to catch the words:

> Shelling peas with a long dress on
> Rockin' in the kitchen, hummin' a song
>
> Fixin' a pot of raindrop tea
> Mint, red clover, and tears from me
>
> Mud on my toes, hair under my arms
> I miss Chopper and all of his charms

The table is covered with a red-and-white checked cloth and set with silverware and mugs. Coffee is perking on the stove. Zimmie is putting together bacon, lettuce, tomato, toast, and mayonnaise at top speed. Isabel feels an astonishing rush of joy. She was hungry. It was so nice for someone to go to that much trouble for her. And she knew, step by step, how much trouble it was. Zimmie laughs as she catches a glimpse of Isabel's face. "What ya thinking about? Christmas?" Isabel ate with enthusiasm, letting Zimmie talk her into sharing a second sandwich. She drinks a lot of coffee, feeling glad the tranquilizers are out of her system, her stomach without the gentle swaying that blunted her appetite. "I never have it this good at home." Isabel laughs, picking up the last bits of bacon with her fingers. Zimmie stacks the dishes in the sink, shoving Isabel away when she tries to wash them. "Leave them! Let them sit and get to know each other awhile. I can wash them when there's nothing more interesting to do." At home Isabel is obsessive about washing a dish as soon as it hits the sink, but she isn't home.

She lets Zimmie lead her back to the living room. Isabel carries over a chair for Zimmie to put her feet up on. "My feet always hurt when I was pregnant," Isabel said, reaching out and massaging Zimmie's toes. "Feels good." Zimmie sinks back on the couch. Isabel has strong fingers. She digs them in under Zimmie's toes, scratches the arch, rubs the heels, loosening her ankles. Once Zimmie relaxes her feet, Isabel works more gently, patting and rubbing, drawing small circles with her thumbnails, tracing the veins; then she massages Zimmie's calves, slapping to force her to unknot the crabapples of muscle.

"Does this mean we're going to make love?" Zimmie asked from way back in the cushion in a teasing voice.

Isabel didn't lose her rhythm. "I haven't made love to a woman since I was twelve. Have you?"

Zimmie toys her tongue against the wall of her cheek. Should she let loose that delicious story? "A few times. I'm not opposed to it. I just don't usually think about sex when I'm with a woman. But I find you very attractive." She watched the blush rise through Isabel's body. She gave a good massage. "Are you faithful to Brian?" Zimmie asked, lying out on the couch so Isabel could reach her back.

"Of course I'm faithful to him. What opportunity do I have, anyway? Should I make love to L., who rubs my ass in the kitchen after I just got through listening to his wife complain that he never lasts long enough for her to have an orgasm? Or to W., who drove me home from a daycare meeting one night and begged me to drive off to Mexico with him and stop at every motel with a view along the way? 'Ahem, I have had a little trouble getting it up lately, but if a woman knows how to touch me just right I'll be fine, and then look out!' No, I've hardly been tempted."

Zimmie was laughing so hard that Isabel let up on her

back, cooling her palms against her cheeks. "Do you and Brian do it every night?" Zimmie asked. She checked Isabel's eyes to see if she minded the question.

"I'm afraid to answer that." She lay her hand on Zimmie's shoulder, pounding with her other fist. "There's the myth that we do it every night and most afternoons. That's for general public consumption. I've had to sit through Brian telling that to his friends. Then there's my version, that we do it two or three times a week and never in the afternoon. And his version that we make love at least five times a week. Once I suggested we keep a chart to see who had the better memory, but Brian waved that aside into the same scrap-heap he puts all my ideas about how to improve our marriage. In truth, if there is such a thing, we do it whenever we can, which means being nice to each other for at least an hour beforehand. Less than we used to, but it's good when we do." Isabel's brow is all screwed up trying to get the different versions out. She and Zimmie are leaning against opposite arms of the sofa, their feet touching under the afghan. The light outside is beginning to filter a gray aura through the curtains. The lamplight inside seems harsh.

"You have a lot more sex in your life than I do," Zimmie says, tugging on the edges of her brown hair. "Before I was twenty I didn't even want sex. I preferred to masturbate; I still get my best orgasms that way."

Isabel couldn't believe that. She'd never even had an orgasm that way. She needed a man for the lightning bolts striking deep in the same place over and over.

"Then when I was twenty I finally got out of the dormitory and went to live on a commune out near the strip. You know Scarecrow, don't you?"

Isabel nods. She's seen him leaning loose and filthy against every wall in town.

"And Charlotte?"

With a girl in a long, patched dress who looked sweetly out of her mind.

"And Charlotte's brother Richard?"

Isabel shrugs. The hippies annoy her because they look like such characters. They wouldn't know her, yet she could probably identify everyone from the area's only country commune.

"This may be Richard's baby. He's in California now. Whew, that was a crazy living situation. So many men and just one other woman. I couldn't get along with Charlotte at all. First off I'd just gotten to·like sex and dropped out of school, and there were four long-haired, suntanned, stoned men sprawling their lazy legs around the house all day. 'I roll joints for a living,' Scarecrow says. He's Charlotte's old man, but when you roll joints for a living you have a lot of free time. That man can really fuck if you catch him before he's too spaced out. He has a tongue as smooth as a sucked-on icicle, but warm. I was sleeping with Scarecrow and with Richard, who was what I call a bouncer in bed; he just crushed me in his arms and let loose so hard, with such a mighty passion, that he swept me away and I didn't mind the lack of skill. Then I got friendly with these other two guys who were supposedly woodworkers, but all they did was get stoned and talk about the furniture they were going to make someday.

"So I was going to bed several times a day: kind of a cram course. Meanwhile Charlotte was into being 'the groovy chick.' She canned, cooked, neatened up the place, swept the incense ashes off the furniture, emptied ashtrays, that sort of stuff. In the evening she put on a long dress and brushed out her long hair and sat around being admired. So you can imagine she didn't like me bouncing around with my big tits in a T-shirt, balling everyone, not caring a damn how I looked or what I wore, no less helping with any of the supposedly woman's work . . . It was really running away from

Charlotte that got me involved with my lesbian friend Milly."

Isabel started back to attention, drifting away from the ghosts in the ditch. Her lesbian friend. Didn't she know Milly too? "Is she the one who spends the afternoon drinking in the Mainliner window and waving to people?"

"Yeah. I talked to her a bunch of times there. She's very nice. We talked about making love until she finally dared me to come up to her room. I can't resist a challenge. We just got undressed in a dispassionate way. It was so different from having to wriggle out of my clothes with a heavy male arm around me. Then she just lay down on the bed and did nothing. She gave me time to explore, touch, find out for myself."

Isabel gets off the couch, wandering around the living room. Her head is being filled with too many sensitive things. Now when she passes Scarecrow hanging on a downtown wall she'd know he had an icicle tongue. When she sees Milly looking out the window . . .

"It shocked me at first to realize how different a woman feels than a man. When you touch a man your hand kind of springs back, but when I touched her my hand sank way in to this incredible softness. . . ."

"That's because women don't develop their muscles," Isabel said. "Feel my arms."

She does have long strips of hardness on her arms. "But you don't have a beard," Zimmie laughs. "Anyway, I just started to touch Milly the way I'd like to be made love to," she strokes Isabel's arm, "until she couldn't stand it anymore. It was fun. It was mainly fun because she was so into it, so turned on, so passionate. Are you turned on, Isabel?"

Isabel was quiet a moment. "I'm more turned on to the conversation than the touching." She settles back on the couch, resting her head on the arm. Zimmie slumps a little. The light glares in their eyes; after a few minutes their lids fall closed.

· · ·

Isabel awoke later to the screeching of birds. Zimmie was asleep, her mouth hanging open. Isabel slipped out of the blanket and searched for her shoes. It was light enough to walk home now. If she left now she'd get back before Brian awoke. She might get away with it after all.

Isabel stepped into the chilly air. She saw lights behind the shades in the three-story houses which had been divided into tiny student apartments. A woman in a housecoat was opening the door for the paper across the street, and way down the block the paper girl returned to her bicycle. The sun wasn't up yet but the sky was light. People got up early in Candle City. They looked healthy with skin freshened by the air and eyes brightened by gazing into the distance of so many sunsets. They had white and red skin and blond hair. Isabel missed New York, missed it indiscriminately, longing for the sight of glass in the street and unbroken rows of buildings. In New York at five thirty a.m. people were straggling home in evening dress. In New York Isabel's blond hair was a sensation. In New York she loved to look into bamboo-colored faces with curly eyelashes, carbon-colored faces with bulging eye sockets, to hear the sweet rain of other languages. In New York . . . she drew herself taller, swinging her arms to impel her body forward . . . everyone walked and talked at top speed. She found the square lawns and triangle houses of Iowa, even the spring flowers crammed into tire beds, dull and alien.

The graduate-student wife. Not much competition. Any Judy with dirty legs standing on the side of the road could lure the bored, graduate-student husband, his eyebrows weary of bending over card catalogues, opening books last checked out in 1943, occasionally writing an erudite letter to someone else in the field. . . . He always asked Isabel to type it for him, though he could type himself; it was one of the things he was nice enough to let her do for him; he liked to make her feel needed.

When she entered her small yellow house, all the lights were on in the living room. Hello, birdcage. The woodwork along the floor and around the doorways was painted robin's-egg blue. She perched her eyes on the several doorways, her skin still tingling from the walk. She checked the children, baby birds safe in their nests, sleeping in their underwear. Brian was sleeping. The stove was crusted with dry tomato sauce. There were toys all over the living-room floor. On the table was a note in Brian's handwriting: "Call your mother."

3

Dear Peanuts, Today was a very boring day and when I say boring I mean boring! The only thing that happened if you want to call it happening was Wendy brought some glitter to school and dumped it all over Larry's hair. Boy when you get that awful glitter in your hair you can't get it out! Hope something happens tomorrow.

Weeks later, on another cool June night, Isabel awoke to the sound of her own dry crying. The light was on. They forgot to cover my cage, she thought. Her diary was open under her cheek, creasing paper and skin. Her neck ached from the twisted sleep. It was one thirty and Brian still wasn't home. She pushed the diary aside, laying her cheek back down on the pillow, sinking into the sway in her stomach, the ahhahh ahhahh baby in her head. The diary fell on the floor. Isabel peeked over the side of the bed.

Dear Peanuts, I know you may think Wendy and I are very bad but I just can't face Hebrew school any longer. We ditched classes and went to Walgreens.

There was a mess on the pink rug: black stretch panties, purple jeans with paint on them, a round embroidered Chinese pillow, a *Newsweek* with Marilyn Monroe in a split-neck black dress, a leaflet on the warning signs of kidney disease. How many years was Marilyn dead and they were still using her bosom to sell magazines? How old was that diary? Her brain stumbled over the calculation. This was 1972. She kept the diary when she was twelve? thirteen? 1955? How old was Marilyn Monroe in 1955? How did that mess get all over the floor? Isabel tried to fall back to sleep without turning the light off. She had taken her fifth Valium at eleven o'clock hoping it would put her out. She's settled into the hammock of the drug, reading her old diary.

Dear Peanuts, I got up at 5 o'clock. We picked up Jerry, "my coach" on the way to Staten Island. I swam the freestyle in 32.1 which I think I could have done better. I swam 40 for the breast stroke but I didn't qualify. Jerry said if I could coordinate I really could go. Well I swam the Butterfly in 34.3 and when my mother found out she flipped.

Mother flipping. How did their mothers always know to call when something was wrong? Or was something always wrong and mothers sometimes called? Or was . . . Isabel giggled. No use twisting her brain. She turned onto her back staring straight up at the offensive hundred-watt lightbulb overhead. "What have you been doing?" her mother asked. "Last time I called Brian said he had no idea where you were." Not nice, Brian. When his mother called tonight and Isabel had no idea where he was, she said, Oh he's at the library working late tonight. Isabel was a soother; Brian was a ruffler. Brian's mother didn't ask hard questions. She inquired about Janey's cold, Marty's toileting, Roy's eating. She wanted to know if Isabel had gone shopping and bought anything for herself lately, remembering that when she was a young mother she never had money or time for shopping. Were they all in good health? Were they going to let the children stay up for the cartoon special on television? Did they need anything? Did the children need anything? They said goodbye, and as she hung up Isabel heard her mother-in-law shout: "Tell Brian his mother loves him," like a battle cry down a thousand miles of telephone wire. Isabel giggled, rolling a little over the side of the bed.

> Dear Peanuts, I went to school. Peter was sure anxious to see me. We're going to the show Saturday. I hope he doesn't try anything cause I don't want to be known as a necker. Mr. Flies told me my grades. F in science and D in math. I hate him. I don't think I deserve such awful grades. Lucky Wendy gets a B in math. But she's also getting an F in science. She and I better study for that test!

I'm going to get right off this bed and clean up the mess on the floor, Isabel thought. Instead, she stretched into a backbend on the rug. Then she stretched up in front of the mirror, rubbing her neck. You're so beautiful, she told the mirror girl with long blond hair and cloudy eyes. She brushed her hair in a slow motion, twisting up the ends. Late at night a woman brushes her hair with moonlight, shivering by an open window, waiting to be moon-burnt, star-bit, night-witched. Was that what she dreamed? Usually beautiful, she murmured. She picked up her black stretch panties and put them in the hamper.

Dear Peanuts, We went over to Wendy's house and went down in the basement. WOW. We danced cheek in cheek! He had his arm around me and told me he liked me. He kept making passes but nothing happened. Boo hoo.

Dear Pea, Today I went to the show. Peter took a long time to get started but he finally got around to it. He kissed me 10 times. The first one was the best one. Nice and long. I got sick and threw up in the girl's room. Then we got kicked out! I haven't yet decided if I like necking with Peter but I just hope I never get sick of him.

She picked up the magazine, walking into the living room to put it on the rack. The lights were on in the living room. It did look like a birdcage. Did she really belong here? If she pushed aside the gold draperies would she see New York? Was that what she dreamed? Why was her neck so sore? She padded back to the bedroom, stooping to pick up the round embroidered Chinese pillow.

Dear Nuts, I just can't decide whether I'm too much in love with Peter or I'm just plain sick of him. I went to shule. I think he feels the same way. When you kiss a boy everything in your life changes. You feel like squeezing him to death. Everytime I think about it I get a funny feeling down below feeling. A feeling like you want to go up and hug him for ever. Bless his little skinny heart.

Isabel placed the pillow carefully in the center of the couch. She noticed that the leaves of her purple passion plant were curled and drooping. The coleus leaves were wrinkling in on themselves. I must be depressed, she thought, I forgot to water the plants. She filled a water glass with a sense of excruciating discipline. I don't feel so depressed. I don't feel that awful. Better living through chemistry. She padded back to the plants. Only the begonias were bright despite her moods, chattering to each other with their tiny white and pink blossoms. She noticed that the turtle's water was seedy but she wasn't up to that. What was she up to? Something before she turned on the faucet, before she spilled the water into the clay pots.

The mess on the bedroom floor. She hesitated over her purple pants, her most comfortable jeans, then pulled them on under her housedress.

> Dear Peanuts, Peter called tonight. Boy do I love that
> kid, even if it was a boring conversation.

The cool breeze beckoned her through the open window. She walked out of the house into the yard. Here we have one great advantage of living in a small town, she told herself, you can just step outside any time you want, any time at all. She sat on the children's swing she'd smoothly painted blue last week. She studied the grass for the track of blue footprints Roy had made after he stepped in the paint can. Meditate, she told herself, rocking back and forth on the narrow swing. Ahhahh baby. What for? she asked herself. To remember your dream, she scolded. Why care? Where was Brian? I'm not going to worry about him. Ridiculous to wish he'd come home when I'm not glad to see him when he does. Probably playing with himself in a ditch; falling asleep in the library.

She climbed onto the low roof behind the garage, scraping her feet against the black tar shingles. Her mind is the surface of the moon: a dark, empty landscape with deep purple craters and volcanoes that smoke yellow in the night.

That was her dream! She tapped her fingers against the gritty shingles.

The yard was very quiet, hedged in on three sides by eight-foot lilac bushes. There was a light shining from the top floor of the house on the right. The old grandfather was up, Isabel noted, wondering if he was sick and sleepless as she. Her mind was a tree branch rapping against a window. What was she doing in this small midwestern town with no friends—Zimmie, she remembered, but Zimmie was precisely the wrong kind of friend for her, Brian said, scowling each time he heard her excited voice on the phone. What was Isabel doing in a small midwestern town when she belonged in New York City? At least in New York City, if one could only find a babysitter, one could eat French food at five in the morning and not be the least disturbed that your husband was out. She could call Zimmie now.

Her mind was a cracked china cup mended with Duco cement. She ran her finger along the fissure of Judy in the Ditch. Healed but scarred. Can minds be mended? Five Valiums today. The doctor wouldn't mind. He would understand if she took just a couple more than the prescription. They were like mama's chicken soup, he said. She was swaying and had to cling to the tar shingles to keep from falling off the roof.

Her mind was the space between the stars. She could meditate on that, and did, staring at the space between two distant bright stars overhead until the black patch of sky pulsed and swelled and sucked her in. She remembered Zimmie's black hole. This must be it, this black blank experience that steadied the swaying. She held the blankness greedily, closing her eyes as it began to spin. When she finally opened her eyes all the stars were falling, every star in the heaven showering down towards her head. She ran inside to call Zimmie.

"I found your black hole."

"You did?"

"It's between two stars right over our garage. I almost fell in. I think I caused some kind of cosmic commotion."

"Uh, Isabel, Chopper came back. We're busy screwing."

Isabel stared into the holes in the white mouthpiece. "Oh, o.k., I just wanted to tell you."

"Are you o.k.?"

"Fine. Perfect."

"I'll call you in the morning."

Isabel walked back to the bedroom, turning out the lights all over the house as she went. She sat down on the bed, picking up her diary, reading the entries she had marked with an asterisk.

Dear Peanuts, Mommy told me Dr. Garden said I craved more attention and affection but not to give me any more than she gave my sister. Richard Moore is in the 8th grade. He's a junior delinquent, likes to neck and looks like a man. I guess I'm sick of everybody and everything, even Peter, which is very rare. Everytime he tried to kiss me I'd start yawning (tee hee). I think I'm going to buy Peter a new ring and just say I found it.

Headlights shone across the bedroom, and she heard the sound of a car pulling into the gravel driveway. The door slammed.

Dear Pea, I went up on stage to sing with my easter hat with the other kids. When it was my turn I got up and I really wiggled. Swivel hips, they called me. Everyone in home room turned around and said "oh Peter." He turned so red he shone. I was teased and teased and teased.

She heard the back door open. Brian stepped heavily across the kitchen, through the swinging door into the living room. She could pretend to be asleep but he must have seen the light on from the driveway.

Dear Peanuts, I'm writing you this from the Keenan Hotel in Fort Wayne, Indiana. Is it neat. I am also writing you with their pen. Diane Fulton and I have our own little room! We're supposed to be in bed. But we aren't. Room number 302. I'm going to beat Diane in the meet tomorrow.

Isabel looked up at Brian, who was unbuttoning his flowered brown and white shirt, his skin glowing beige. He's so good-looking, she thought, the sight of him lighting a neon path around her stomach which ended in a sharp clench of desire high in her womb. Like a tall sugarcane with a top hat of brown hair. It was true that their marriage was based on sex. Once Isabel heard a lecturer make fun of teenagers who married just because of sex, and her thought was "What else is there?" and she hadn't yet discovered.

"Why don't you throw that old diary away?" Brian said, peeling off his shirt and dropping it on a chair. "The cover's coming off, the ink is smeared, it's all ruined."

"Where ya been?" Her voice sounded slurred.

"I had some things to take care of."

"Your mother called."

"Oh, yeah? What'd she have to say?"

Isabel was watching the black curls of hair on his chest, and his hips emerging from his beige dungarees. "She said, 'Tell him his mother loves him.' " Brian laughed. "And how are the kids and all. Oh, and Arnie and Carla are getting divorced and your aunt is throwing herself out the window over it."

He sat next to her on the bed, tugging at his socks.

Dear Peanuts, Seems like the days are getting shorter and shorter. The summer is whizzing by. Then comes winter. I hate winter. Slush all over the sidewalks, the trees waving their ugly branches at me.

"Would you stop reading that damn thing!" Her shoulders jolted; she put the diary in the small drawer of her night table and slumped back on the bed. "Arnie and Carla, huh? Did you tell her mazeltov?"

"I got the feeling they'd been separated for a long time, but your aunt kept it a secret."

"If she told my mother, it's no longer a secret." He kneeled on the bed, looking down at her as she huddled deeper in the covers. "Izzy, it's not that cold."

"Turn off the light."

He tugged the blanket down around her shoulders. She was still wearing her housedress and purple jeans. "Aren't you going to get undressed? You really are stoned out, honey."

She shielded her eyes. "Turn off the light or get me my sunglasses."

He undressed her quickly, as if he were stripping a bed, thought Isabel, which he never did because Isabel did that. One of these days she was going to raise the question of housework with Brian. And the question of staying out so late and where did he go and how come. One of these days they'd be on speaking terms again. Did she say mazeltov about Arnie and Carla, indeed. He threw the covers over her and turned off the light.

Isabel stretched out on her hammock, carefully adjusting her body to minimize the swaying and perfect the balance. The air around Brian was cold from the outdoors. His fingers poked against her clitoris, oops, she started at the touch, then rolled slightly to leave room for him on the now rocking hammock. Her vagina responded warmly, while her mind pitched and the ceiling spun and her back hurt against the hammock strings. "I love you," she said, opening her eyes, hearing her words echo down the years until they reached him and he grimaced. He replied by quickening the crashing inside her. "I don't know what love is," he had said to her often, and she figured he was right. She felt from Brian's intensified pounding that he was about to come and remembered to practice that quick flexing of her lower muscles that began a momentary orgasmic spasm in her: clutch, clutch, clutch, moan, release. Brian rolled off her, smiling, pleased that they had come together.

Then, instead of sleeping, Isabel remained strung a foot above their queen-sized bed, her thighs quivering like twin tuning forks. The dark blue light coming through the window shades kept her eyes awake. She was aware of every passing hour in alarm-clock orange glowing from the dresser. She saw 2:30 and 3:15 and 4:25. She wasn't awake enough to move her limbs or get up and drink milk to soothe her parched throat. Her thoughts were not anxious. My body is asleep, I'm getting the rest I need. She swayed, riding the five tranquilizers until they finally drifted out of her body in the first glare of daylight. The strings of the hammock slipped. Her body fell gently onto the firm mattress beside Brian's back. The mattress didn't move at all; there was no swaying. She lay her cheek against Brian's bare back and fell asleep.

4

Are you a hippie or a radical?
That's what I gotta know
A pot-head or a militant
Which way you gonna go?

Isabel picked up the phone. "I knew it was you."

"Sorry I couldn't talk last night."

"You must be so happy he's back."

"Uh, moderately, moderately. He's o.k. I'm fond of the guy. He's still sleeping, of course. I told him all about you and he can't wait to meet you."

"Hold on a minute." Isabel led the children into the living room and turned on the t.v. "Zimmie, what could you possibly have told him about me that would make him want to meet me?"

"Oh, that you were so open to things and had real strong feelings. Stuff like that. Listen, Iz, Chopper says he wants to video-tape the birth. I'm going to try to talk the doctor into letting him."

"Zimmie, the hell with video tape, you need someone to *help* you."

"Would you do it?" I mean if the doctor said o.k., would you be there?"

"Oh yes. I'm so excited. Oh! Yes!"

"At first I didn't want anyone there, in case I freaked out, but once I got to know you I figured either you wouldn't mind or you'd freak out right along with me."

"You'll get through it fine. You've got a lot of guts. Are you sure Chopper won't take off again?"

"Pretty sure. He's more reliable than I make out; I'm a

terrible pessimist. But you know he did meet a rich blond girl in Aspen. He was attracted to her because she called her father a capitalist swine, but then she hung out in his tent sweeping it out and tidying it up while he went fishing and he got tired of watching her taking care of him rather than trying to have a good time herself. Well, if that's settled, I got to get off."

Isabel yanked the extra-long phone cord from Roy, who was gumming it. "When am I going to see you? We should practice the breathing together."

"When can you get out?"

"Never. Why don't you come over tonight? I'm so excited!"

"Of course you are, Isabel. It's gonna be incredible for you guys. I'm the one who's gonna sweat."

Isabel lined up three sets of clothing on the living room floor and called her troop together. Janey managed to pull her clothes on by herself, and Isabel ignored the backwards polo shirt. Marty made good progress with his socks and dungarees under the gentle fountain of Isabel's instructions. But Roy, almost two, struggled against the undershirt, wiggled out of his pants, and finally had to be spanked into a spurt of stillness long enough for Isabel to tie his sneakers. All the while Isabel was pulsing at the thought of seeing a birth. If she had to reduce her life to three days she'd choose the birth days of her children. With each she'd been too absorbed and exhausted to look into the overhead mirrors. She'd closed her eyes at the delivery-room glare.

Isabel was breathing hard by the time she had the kids in the back of the Volkswagen. Their faces, newly scrubbed, gleamed at her bright as sunspots on blue water. As she drove she ran through her pregnancies again, remembering the first with a big splash of attention from Brian: he did the heavy housework and grocery shopping while she took naps; he took her out to dinner, to the movies whenever she suggested it. Her second pregnancy was met with less indulgence, more restlessness on his part, but then the product turned out to be "a boy," which thrilled Brian's parents and made Brian revere Isabel for months as if it showed some special womanly talent on her part. The third pregnancy, ah, that was played to a diminishing audience. Isabel's mother objected: "I was satisfied with two, and I had both girls." Brian was annoyed, commenting that at least it would keep Isabel occupied and off his back.

Isabel braked suddenly and the children flew forward: "You have to drive more carefully, Mommy," Janey said gravely. She was going to tell Zimmie the truth, just say it right out: it hurts, Zimmie. None of this "there's only a little discomfort" business. Isabel paled at the memory of the transition between the gathering contractions and the sudden, earth-shattering desire to expel the baby. It was that moment of terrified realization that if it got any worse you really couldn't stand it that made women call for the shot of Demerol which left them dulled and helpless during what Isabel thought was the best part.

The children jumped out of the car and ran towards the daycare yard. Isabel walked slowly behind them, greeting the other children. "Hello, Benja-menjin. Hello, Christo-burger. Hello, Anna Banana." Their faces were all dirty. Christopher had a running nose. Anna's diaper was drooping. Isabel shuddered at the mess. Tomorrow was her day to work; she'd try to clean the toys, spray out the diaper smell from the air, wash the greasy linoleum. The lack of funds and time and the sudden dips in enthusiasm which plagued the cooperative kept the parents from giving immaculate, sanitary care. Isabel reconciled herself. The children were all smiling and playing. Even Roy didn't protest when she closed the door and set off to work.

As she drove through Candle City, skillfully maneuvering her direction despite the row of No Left Turns that used to beguile her, she wondered at the strong feeling in her chest and thighs. Her blood was percolating. Had she brought her tranquilizers? She was so used to feeling their rocking numbness that any other sensation surprised her. Zimmie's call, she remembered, that's what she was so happy about. How should she put it to Brian? Her arms were trembling as she pulled on her racing suit near the row of green lockers. Don't ruin it, Isabel. Don't just burst out in a storm of talk about the great good news, because he won't see it that way. It doesn't include him. Why should Isabel be excited about something that doesn't revolve around Brian? She'd have to tell him casually, in an off-handed manner. Oh by the way, this is kind of a drag but I don't know how to get out of it. Remember the night you told me about your motorcycle affair? Begin by blowing up a few guilty hairs on his neck. Zimmie was talking about being all alone when she had her baby and I said, if she couldn't find anyone else that I would go to the hospital and stay with her. Well, today she called and asked if I would do it for sure. I'm not too ecstatic about the idea. . . .

Isabel tugged the tight swimming cap around her hair. She could hear the children shouting at the edge of the pool. I'm disgusting, she thought, plotting against my own husband. The guilt settled in like a low fog. She could barely breathe. There was a small bottle of Valium in the top of her locker. She had taken five yesterday, so she'd only take two today, she bargained, swallowing two pills and feeling immediately calmer. She walked in long strides out of the locker room and dove off the side of the pool. The water splashed over her in an aqua chlorine chill. She swam two laps in her powerful crawl until her body warmed up. The children were shouting among themselves as she bobbed up over the side. "Line up. I want to see everybody wet."

Zimmie hesitated before Isabel's door, trying to set the words to her song:

Are you a hippie or a radical?
There's a difference I've been told
Are you satisfied just getting stoned?
Or do you . . .

She couldn't get the last line, hadn't been able to on her whole walk across town. She wanted to be able to deal with the collision she felt was coming with Chopper; she remembered the look on his face when he found she'd smoked up his two ounces of grass while he was away. He hadn't brought it up last night, but she knew he would at some point. The day they met, both expelled by the courts, practically colliding on the courthouse steps, they decided to put their heads together: How to lead a revolutionary life? How to avoid the twin perils of corruption and assimilation? They were always hammering at the questions, laughing at their fumbling failure to answer them:

Are you satisfied just getting stoned?
Will you change before you're old?

She didn't like the line. Everyone changed. She rang Isabel's bell.

The house was a shock to Zimmie; it didn't look like the poor-student quarters she expected. There was wall-to-wall gold carpeting, a heavy blond dining room set, a long brown couch, golden draperies. Zimmie let Janey and Marty press their small hands against her belly, kissing them before Isabel pushed them off to bed.

Are you a hippie or a radical?
There's a difference I've been told
Are you satisfied just getting high
Watching history unfold?

Or do you want to fight to change things
To end the exploitation
To reimburse the working class
And found a hippie nation?

Zimmie laughed at her own confusion. She was wearing cut-off jeans tied together with a rope, the zipper open to leave room for her stomach. Her Pakistani print smock covered all but the frayed edges of her shorts in bright red medallions. She looked squash-shaped to herself in the reflection in the plate-glass window. Funny-looking as usual.

Isabel came out of the children's room, threatening a spanking if she heard one more peep. She didn't look well. Her eyes were as cloudy as a bottle of ammonia. She walked about the living room touching things: the childbirth paperbacks she'd arranged on the glass coffee table; the Indian sand painting over the secretary; the white star daffodils cut from the row on the side of the house. "Where'd you get all this furniture?" Zimmie asked abruptly.

"Brian's parents are very generous," Isabel said. She looked at a point way beyond Zimmie's shoulder, as if there was a black hole out there sucking her attention with its gravity. "His mother especially: 'You do your job, darling, and you'll have everything you want. Everything. I agree that you should have as many children as you want. Three, four. Why, my niece Carla has four children and she still manages to teach kindergarten and put her husband through medical school. No sacrifice is too much for a Jewish wife. Look at me—do I ask anything for myself? Only the best for my children.' "

Zimmie was amused at Isabel's switch into a Jewish accent. Isabel seemed mesmerized by her thoughts, standing in the middle of the gold carpet, her brown skirt and sweater set off against the gold-threaded curtain. Finally, with a snap of her head: "How are you feeling, Zimmie?"

Zimmie checked carefully. The results were discouraging. Her breasts were heavy, aching underneath. Her groin muscles tickled metallically under the weight of her stomach. The rope holding her shorts together was rough against her skin. She felt warm in the face, under the arms, between the breasts. "It better be this week. This baby wants out."

They did some breathing exercises: pants, shallow surface breaths, blows. Zimmie refused to do the leg lifts. Too much trouble. She was exasperated by Isabel's remoteness. Where were the fast-flowing tears, the sudden smiles? She couldn't catch Isabel's eyes. Zimmie lifted her heavy breasts with her hands to let some air under them. Noticing this, Isabel drew out of her cloud a moment; what did it feel like to have such big breasts to hold whenever you liked?

"I was looking forward to coming here all day," Zimmie said aloud, after rehearsing the sentence. "I didn't think you'd be so spaced out."

Isabel was staring into the center of a daffodil. "What?"

"How come you're so spaced out?"

"Oh, I'm just relaxed. I've been having so much trouble with Brian that I've had to take more Valiums every day to keep things mellow."

"Still worrying about the girl in the ditch?"

"Oh no. Yeah. A little. Other things, too. . . . All I ask is a little thanks for all the things I do for him."

Zimmie sighed, relaxing into the chocolate-covered sofa. "You can't thank someone enough for sacrificing her life."

Isabel struggled up in the yellow armchair. "There was one thing I really wanted to tell you about. Transition." Her voice was thick. She should never have taken those two . . . four . . . Why had she forgotten how great it was to be with Zimmie? Why was she taking those pills all the time as if they were Pez? She had questioned herself briefly as she swallowed two more at dinnertime. It wasn't as if she were committing suicide. It helped her cope with Brian complaining about the

Indians and the reheated dinner. She wanted to avoid a quarrel at all costs. If they argued, he'd be too upset to go back to the library. Another evening lost, another demerit for the graduate-student wife, that much longer to spend in the abominable role of suffering a provincial existence in Candle City. If he/she failed to get the degree and get out . . . Zimmie was looking at her expectantly.

"What's transition?"

"Oh. You'll read about it in the book. Transition is the hardest time. It just gets worse and worse, then the urge to push starts and it gets easier."

Zimmie shrugged in annoyance. What mumbly gook. Maybe she'd been too hasty about Isabel. What help would she be? Mama Alp would be better off pushing baby Alp out all by herself. She began to fold the piles of baby clothes Isabel had given her. They heard Brian's car pulling up.

"Well, ladies." Brian kissed Isabel full on the lips. She kept her hands at her sides, barely lifting her arms. "How are you feeling, Izzy? Got your temper back? Hello, mommy," he said to Zimmie. Their glances struck flint, sparking. "Have you had any dope yet?" He opened the carved rosewood box on the mantel, rolling a joint.

"Get any work done?" Isabel asked. His eyes hopped over his shoulder from Isabel to Zimmie. His gestures reminded Zimmie of the tipped balance of a mobile that wobbled in the slight breeze of Isabel's question. "Why do you ask?" he said finally. Isabel hit the chair softly with her fists.

Chopper rang the bell, calling for Zimmie. Isabel watched him with a dim curiosity as he squeezed Zimmie from behind, rubbing her lemon-shaped belly. His hair was tightly braided at the sides of his head, glistening brown with sweat. He was still wearing the dungarees and T-shirt he'd been playing baseball in. There was a large embroidered zero on his shirt. He smelled of the playing fields, standing easily on his curled-tongue sneakers for the introductions.

Brian banged the rosewood box shut. "Are you still in school?" he asked Chopper. He had seen him in the halls with other girls than Zimmie.

"I'm taking some media courses, but actually I'm a professional revolutionary." He glanced at Zimmie, holding his lips straight to suppress a smile.

"Aw gosh, Chopper, what a hero, humble too."

Brian smiled brightly, his mustache wiggling as he licked the joint closed. Isabel's hands were knotted in fists. Got her temper back, indeed. "You can't be a revolutionary in America," Brian said. "The system won't let you. In other countries they'll either kill you or put you in power, but the genius of the American system is assimilation. It's not true that everyone has his price. But those who don't can always get a job working for Vista. The more radical they are the quicker they get promoted, until they've got such a stake in the middle class they forget about burning and pillaging and start saving for their vacations."

"Is that what your dissertation is about?" Chopper asked. He sat next to Zimmie, watching Isabel, who was sitting poised and stiff as a model set down to show off the furniture and advertise her mid-calf brown skirt.

"No, no. I'm writing up part of the oral tradition of the Emotin Indians in this county." He unearthed his portable tape recorder. "I got this baby on a grant from the graduate college." He turned it on and they listened to a grave voice telling a story about squirrels and sparrows. He flicked it off. "I'm finished with most of the collecting. I have about five good tales and a lot of fragments. My teacher is very excited about it. It's so important to get these stories written down before they're lost." He lit the joint and passed it with a flourish to Zimmie.

"Those stories must have been around a long time," she said. "What makes you think they'll get lost?"

"The Indians are getting acculturated," Brian said; Chopper raised a shaggy eyebrow. "They watch too much television. Anyway, there's a lot of publishers interested in Indian books right now. My teacher said I might be able to cash in on it if I can get the book ready before the next fad takes hold. But all that depends on my dear wife holding up her end," he finished, locking gazes with Isabel. Zimmie was getting dizzy watching the marble game of glances between the four of them. She tried to get closer to Chopper on the couch, but his arm was wet.

"How did you get the Indians to tell you the stories?" Chopper asked.

"Oh, they're anxious to. They want the teachings spread around. The old man who told me most of them was thrilled to have an audience." He laughed suddenly. "His grandson, a kid in a college sweatshirt, offered to tell me stories at two dollars an hour."

"Did you pay him?"

"Oh, no. I'm sure he didn't know any stories."

Zimmie tried to pass the joint to Isabel but she refused. She gave it to Chopper, who handed it back to Brian.

"Don't you smoke?"

"I gotta get home now." Chopper bounced up on his sneakers. "I think I'll write an editorial about this academic rip-off of Indian culture. I bet that kid had a lot more interesting stuff to say than his grandfather."

Zimmie watched Brian: the mobile was spinning crazily from Chopper's remark, his arms fumbling with the joint, the ashtray, as he tried to stand up. "You know, I raised the same objections to my adviser when he first suggested the topic. But he explained that the teachings would all be lost if it weren't for the diligence of the academic community. Besides, these Indians live right in this county, and local topics are encouraged at a state university." He opened the door for them. "Besides, it's all relative anyway. It was nice meeting you."

"They hated me," Brian said when they were gone.

"Worse than that, Zimmie hated me tonight," she said. "And I love her. I shouldn't have taken all those pills. I couldn't . . ."

"Skip the existential drama, Izzy." He sat on the floor next to her chair, relighting the joint. "The doctor said you should take them." He was quiet a moment, drawing the smoke in deeply, then dropped the shredded roach into an ashtray and reached up, stroking Isabel's arm. "Do you still love me?"

"In my spare time, when I have a free moment."

"I have something to tell you that you're not going to like."

"You broke another Thermos."

He kept his eyes on his knees. "I've been having an affair. I was trying to tell you about it weeks ago, but I blurted out that stupid motorcycle story instead. The girl is very young, she means nothing to me. She's kind of a bitch." Is he saying this or am I imagining it? Isabel thought. "I don't love her or anything. I only love you, my wife. But I've been seeing quite a bit of her. The reason I'm telling you about it is she's pregnant. I need to take four hundred dollars out of our account to pay for her airfare and abortion in New York. I could have asked my mother for the money, but I felt . . ."

The hammock strings snapped. Isabel found herself flailing about in a net, her face pressed into her knees, barely able to twist her face to the side so she could breathe. She struggled to tip the net. She wanted to fall to the ground with a thud, to feel the collision. Brian's eyes were wet and dark as he reached for her shoulders, pulling her to their bed. Her arms and legs waved in the air, threads lifted on air current. He brought her a pill and a glass of water. She felt the soothing swaying renew.

"Are you all right?"

"Go to hell," she said. She curled herself into a knot and fell asleep.

5

Isabel got out of bed, curling her toes as they touched the floor. She faced the day with a question mark. It was just dawn but her eyes felt pasted open. She was up. Brian was tossing heavily in the bed, groping for her on the still-warm sheet. She wondered which way the day would go. If Brian touched her shoulder, even by accident, if he gave her a slight smile, an easy nod; if they weren't out of milk, coffee, bread, eggs, or butter and she got the eggs perfect, didn't burn the toast or boil the coffee; if Janey, Marty, and Roy ate their cereal peacefully without smearing raisins on Brian's newspaper—the door of happy memories would swing open. "I found my thrill, on blueberry hill." She would hand him the bankbook with an understanding nod. If he got out the door without a word said about it, if she could keep a neutral expression on her face as he left the house, then ran back for his keys, then ran back for his briefcase, then ran back to change his jacket and have just a small poke of hashish in the closet, and finally the car started and the Volkswagen zipped out of view, she'd have a good day. If Brian got out o.k., no matter what happened later, Isabel was fine. She'd spend the morning playing Mozart records, vacuuming down a checkerboard lane shaded by golden oak trees. The children's noise would seem like singing. When they fought she'd muse, "They learn from this too."

But—she sat down again at the foot of the bed—if the first thing in the morning there was a rough phrase: "This coffee tastes like cleanser." "Are we out of butter again? Didn't I go shopping for you yesterday?" (for *me?*)—the door of dissonance would blow open. "Women is losers, women is losers." He could find the bankbook himself. She could pay for her own abortion. And if, then, the car wouldn't start and he came back to the house for a rag to wipe off the distributor cap, found the kids fighting, Isabel leaning against the refrigerator with lakes of water ready to flow from her eyes; if the day were damp and their Sierra Club posters slumped on taped corners, the kitchen smelled of sweetened milk and soggy cereal, and he said, "You look like hell, Isabel. Why don't you get a suntan?"—all the fights they'd ever had would ring in her ears. All the unkind things he'd said to her. His complaints would lodge on her eyebrows and lump her shoulders. The kids would sound like screeching cats. She'd push the vacuum down a mud road cracked and baked by an orange sun. She'd take aspirins, amazed it was only ten thirty.

In any case, it was not up to her. She got off the bed again, her toes curling like question marks as they touched the cold floor. It was just after dawn.

She walked to the bathroom, looking absently in the mirror. Then she took another, deeper look. Her hands flew to her cheeks in alarm. Her cheeks had collapsed into deep pits diving towards her suddenly pointed chin. Had she lost so much weight in her face? Lines, like rock seams, ridged her forehead. Her eyes were shored with wide purple circles. She pressed closer to the mirror. Is that what she looked like? Her skin slack, the color of cooked cereal, her eyes looking weakly back at her like they'd never see again. "I'm forty!" she cried, pressing her nose against the mirror, pulling on her hair, still gold and fluffy along the edges of her beach-wrecked face. How did it happen? She'd lost all those years. Were the children grown up? Is that why she woke before them? Were they off in college? Forty. What about the thirties, when she planned to loosen up and enjoy life? She found black lines on her upper eyelids, as if she'd purposely used eyeliner to make herself up as a witch. Forty! Maybe she was actually dead. Her throat ached as if it were strangling itself from within. She slumped to the bathroom floor, her hands still dangling under the running cold water in the sink. She felt awful. Had she never thought of death before? Of aging? Brian . . . The strangling throat laughed. Was that Brian's department too, or was she going to have to die alone, on her own, just as he and the kids . . . How could she be thinking these things? Her eyes were closed on a terrible darkness. She who cringed at making out a will and left it all to Brian. She tried to pull herself up, but got more tangled in the pipes under the sink, closing her eyes at the hairy nest near the base of the toilet. A golden ball exploded in the darkness beneath her eyelids.

Very slowly, like a thought coming from another mind, she knew what was wrong with her. She had seen that golden ball before when she took too many pills. But never such a shattering brightness. The pills. The thought pulled her off the floor; she leaned on the sink. Yes, she still looked forty. She might be restored. It was only the touch of death, not the real thing. She took out her small vial of tranquilizers and spilled the frisky yellow pills into her palm. She turned her hand over neatly, landing the pills in the toilet bowl. She flushed. Kaboom!

I just did something, she thought. The hollow-faced girl in the mirror didn't look glad, but the strangling in her throat was relieved. Is that o.k., Brian? It better be, for she felt herself startlingly new, as if the pain caught up with her, sucking her into its black hole, reversing all her directions.

O.k. She might be o.k. Roy's baby cry came from the children's room. She walked slowly to him, trying to hold the puppet pieces of her face together.

> I'm an odd sort of woman
> I really want to talk to you
> So don't smile at me lady
> When crying's what you want to do

Zimmie sagged in the clinic waiting room like an oversized plastic bag with leaves settled towards the bottom. She had been waiting two hours. Two hours! Two hours in a molded plastic chair. Her eyes swept across the row of plastic chairs facing her. They were stuffed with pregnant women who managed tiny smiles if they saw her looking. When the nurse finally called their names, their smiles peeled open as they gathered their bags and rushed towards the changing room—good Christians rushing to their just reward. The doctor will see you now. Five minutes in his restorative presence. Your turn has come.

There were only two ahead of her now. Zimmie occupied her mind keeping careful track of her turn. There was the young farm girl wearing a white maternity dress printed with tiny pink and blue flowers. She wore a gold wedding band and a tiny diamond ring on her swollen fingers. Sweet as a warm day in the woods. If I were a man I'd probably be just reactionary enough to marry someone like her.

Across from Zimmie was a country woman of a different class. She looked fifty: a starved horse with a wrinkled hide, hanging breasts, and a jaw that, since it had no teeth, swallowed her lips instead. She had a couple of children with thin, quaking legs jumping up and down near her chair until one gathered the momentum to run to the other side of the waiting room, shoot a scared look down the hall, and dash back to his mother's side. The woman told Zimmie she was only thirty-two. "It's the teeth that make me look older." Zimmie made a brief, angry statement about the rotten capitalist system which allowed people to be so poorly fed their teeth fell out prematurely. The woman leaped back from the words. "I'm not saying it's your fault." Zimmie reached across to touch her hand. The woman looked at Zimmie's fingers. "Are you married, honey? Well, I guess I'm luckier than some."

Two hours and fifteen minutes! Part of the reason she took the waiting so badly was her shame at her own inactivity. If she could only organize these women. The whole clinic was run for the doctors. They told everyone to come at nine a.m. as if women had all the time in the world to numb their bottoms on molded plastic seats. On the floor near her foot she glanced, again, at the portrait of a government couple on the cover of a newsmagazine. The man gazed ahead at the Capitol; his wife's face was turned in half profile, looking up at her husband. Zimmie stepped on the magazine, mashing it with her sandal.

"Zimmie Alp." It was her turn. She lay back on the examining table, closing her eyes from the white cabinets filled with instruments and bottles. I have a right to have this baby. If the IUD had done its job, if the quinine had worked, you would never have made it this far, Che Guevara Alp. Be proud and fearless. You've already defeated the worst odds. "I'll marry you," Richard said. "I like you pretty well. You have the makings of a groovy chick." It was easy enough turning him down: "Bad enough the kid might have your genes, Richard; let's spare him your upbringing." But what was she going to put on the birth certificate? Oh, if only Isabel comes through on that day of days. Isabel seemed less dependable than Chopper. It was only she herself.

Ah, she hated all this thinking that was creeping up on

her with motherhood. She always got into reviewing her situation when she came to the clinic. She wanted to remain a child: plan the act, do it, get away with it.

Nineteen hundred and sixty-eight
Was a long exciting year
The revolution didn't hesitate
There was no such thing as fear

She would make a perfect henchman. Thinking irritated her. It was so much less pleasant than being stoned. Chopper was proud of her working-class background, but he pushed her to think, analyze, explain herself, as if she spent all day in the classroom like he did.

"Good morning." Dr. Crinose smiled, motioning her feet down into the stirrups.

"You mean it isn't lunchtime yet?"

"Move down a little more. More. That's it. I delivered two babies this morning. They didn't have appointments. How is it you're the only patient who complains about waiting?" He pressed down on her stomach.

They're all mares, dolts, breeders. Zimmie swallowed. "Maybe I'm the only one who has the guts."

He peered delicately up her. "You're not dilated, but I think the head is engaged. It may be soon. If not, I'll see you next week."

Zimmie rose in the stirrups. "Uh, wait a minute, I want to ask you something."

He stood in the doorway with his head cocked towards her. "I'd like to have a friend in the delivery room with me. You know, kind of helping and keeping me company. She's had three babies, so . . ."

"She . . ."

"She's experienced in this method. Also another friend of

mine is taking a course in video-taping and he'd like to film the birth."

"He . . ."

"He'll have a Portopak camera that won't get in the way or need special lights or equipment."

The nurse was urging him on to the next booth. He stood for a moment, rubbing his black beard, watching Zimmie inch back on the table, the gown wrinkling under her, the paper crunching. "Wait for me in my office," he said, vanishing.

Brian had taken the car, so Isabel walked back from her swimming class in the late afternoon. Her hair was damp and annoying on her back. The sun disappeared slowly behind a green mist. A hundred times during the day she had reached for a tranquilizer, then remembered. I'll be ready when Zimmie calls, she thought. The air was warm and soft on her cheeks. As she walked across the long campus she kept passing herself. There she was, twenty years younger, in a plaid pleated skirt showing off kicky legs. There she was on exam day, when she hadn't washed her long hair in a while, just stuck on that old red sweater and ran with her notes jammed into a textbook. The rising humidity was forming dense clouds which cast a ghoulish yellow-green light on the passing faces. There she was with sun-colored curvy hair, walking double-fast to keep up with the long striding boy who talked intensely down at her.

When Isabel reached the house she walked straight to the mirror above the bathroom sink. She looked a little better than this morning. Her eyes glinted back at her. Outside the rain began to fall in big drops. She circled the house, closing windows, then came back to her reflection. Her cheeks were still pitted. She pointed to the lines on her forehead. Her long hair seemed an absurd reminder of lost youth. She walked to the kitchen drawer, took out the shears she used to cut chicken in pieces, and hurried back to the mirror. She grabbed a front hank, cutting a great gash of hair off over her ear. The scissors jammed on the hair, and she had trouble pulling them open. The other side came out a little longer, but not quite as crooked. She pulled sections of the back hair forward, twisting them over her shoulder. In three more hacks she had short hair. Kaboom! She put a wet brush through her hair, watching the ends curl up as they'd done when she was eleven, the last time she'd had short hair. She looked in the mirror in relief. She was no longer the prettiest girl in the class. No golden mane to mock her forty years. Brave girl. She patted herself on the shoulder with two fingers, as she used to do when she won a swimming meet. The sink was full of hair.

Dr. Crinose squeaked back in his revolving chair. "It's all right with me. As long as you don't expect to smoke marijuana in the delivery room, I don't mind your friends."

Zimmie opened up her smile to him. "That's super."

"You're refreshing," he said. "You've enjoyed being pregnant, eh? I think you'd better talk to Dr. Shote about the filming, so he can alert the nursing staff. His office is right down the hall. Maybe you should say the man is your husband." He winked.

Zimmie shuddered. "Look, I have nothing against lying in some situations, but that would be licking the dust. I'll never be married."

"Ah—never. What will you do when you're thirty-five? You'll be all alone."

"I'm all alone now. So are a lot of married people. My friend has agreed to be the male-image for the kid for a while, as long as he doesn't call him Daddy."

She didn't have to wait for Dr. Shote. He was sitting at a long desk dealing out papers and magazines. He heard her out with the air of one who always hears the other person

pillow under her until the baby settled, pulling the tendons of her back so that she had to switch sides. She kicked her numbing legs in frustration, waking Chopper, who joked, "Will you tell that kid to stop kicking me?" He ran his hands over her back and neck, trying to soothe her, but her hot skin was quickly irritated by any touch, and finally she asked him to move to his own bed, and he rose sleepily. Then she was alone, glaring at the ceiling with hot tears in her eyes. Zimmie the earth mother: swollen, muddy, furious.

"What do you see in me, Chopper?" she asked him months ago, and memorized his reply, using the sentences now to clobber down her despair. "You're a fighter, you're funny, you're great in bed, you're always up for an adventure, you have no sense of responsibility—" "That you like?" "It's a fault, but I like it. You're like a firefly lighting up unexpected places in the night for me. But best of all I like myself when I'm with you. I'm funnier. And I feel so revolutionary with you holding my arm in solidarity."

Zimmie smiled at the memory. Ah, she knew rationally she'd get her strength back, she'd be able to run from cops again, roll in sexual passion again, sleep on her stomach again. But now the weakness was pervasive, it was forever. It sucked the energy from her other selves. Zimmie the ladybug turned on her back in the hospital corridor with six legs kicking.

Dr. Crinose shot past her. She grabbed at his white coat. "Listen! I've been waiting for you for hours. Would you please talk Dr. Shote into allowing the video-taping? He doesn't find me as refreshing as you do."

Brian and the children got home a few minutes after Isabel, shaking rain over the rug, hurling themselves against her silence. "Your hair—" Brian said in a burst, "How could you do . . . your hair was your loveliest . . . you look like an ordinary housewife now. You did it on purpose!"

How could she? On purpose. As he spoke she felt the desire for a tranquilizer like a baby doll in her chest saying "mama" each time it was squeezed. Janey touched the points of her mother's hair. "Cut mine off too! Does it hurt to cut your hair?"

Isabel rattled into the dinner preparations. Brian watched her sideways down the galley kitchen. The way he looks at the garbage disposal when it's stuffed, analyzing the dysfunction, Isabel thought. He sidestepped the children, motioning them towards Isabel for shoelace-tying and nose-wiping. She wanted a pill. She wanted something to sway her gently away, to steady her as the children crawled between her legs like vermin and Brian shrank before her eyes. Brian the pillar, the tower: if she wasn't married to him she'd be married to someone else. Brian the tall poplar tree, slim and rising, rooted to a slope, whom she always wanted to wrap her arms around and around, holding on through electric storms and torrents. She shook off the children and they wailed and complained, but she hardly heard them, thinking of her first sight of Brian, wondering if she'd ever looked at him since the first image of him walking in his sweater, swinging books on his long long arm, under the campus trees right before a rain, had filled her with a desire to wrap herself around him. Casually his arm reached across the seat of his car to accept her, across miles of telephone wires, across a two-month separation and a vow never to be apart again, across two more years of college until the wedding the wedding.

She wasn't used to the rush of thoughts, pausing with a half-sliced onion in her hand. Mama, I need a pill, she thought in the lapse, then flashed on an image of the frontispiece of her diary:

Favorite color . . . . . Yellow
Famous person . . . . Joan of Arc

Best quality .... Courage
Favorite car .... Chevrolet
Secret ambition .... Gold Medal Olympic Swimmer

Was that eleven-year-old girl still throbbing in her scarred forty-year-old body? Why hadn't she become a champion swimmer? Thinking back she couldn't remember a single serious obstacle. "Boy crazy," her mother used to say.

She tried to shift into action, assembling the hamburgers, french fries, and stringbeans on three small Mickey Mouse plastic plates and one platter for Brian. Why this looking back and back and setting herself a-tremble? Think ahead, she recommended, marching back and forth from the kitchen to dining table with bottles of ketchup, mustard, pickles, and grape juice in three plastic mugs and iced coffee for Brian. The most exciting thing would be Zimmie's childbirth. There was something to look forward to. How could meeting Zimmie be such an important thing in her life? It didn't make sense. What Greek goddess met a new girlfriend and changed her life? None. It didn't appear in any popular songs.

She sat down at the table, chin on two fists, looking out the window at the pounding rain. "Aren't you eating, Mommy? Daddy, why isn't Mommy eating?"

"Isabel?"

She had been rash to toss those pills out. This dinner—she'd never make it through, but if she fled the table, the children would be disturbed and not eat and Brian and all her work, all those fixings neatly arranged on the red-and-white checked tablecloth, all the right American food, the shrunken, plump hamburgers Brian had made on the grill under the garage roof, despite the rain. "In a while," Isabel said, thinking of the yellow pills floating around and around in the toilet bowl as it flushed. No matter. She could always get some more. She plunked a glob of ketchup on Marty's plate, not noticing he hadn't touched the other pool. "I don't like stringbeans," Janey said, putting them one by one on the table. "Isabel, would you look what she's doing?"

What was she thinking before . . . That was the trouble with kids, they never let you think or daydream. When she looked back to the table the children were gone, their plates full of food, except baby Roy's; he seemed to have eaten everything—or was it that he mashed it onto his highchair tray? Brian was reading the university newspaper. The rain stopped suddenly and the sun was bright on the wet grass. Isabel rapidly cleared the litter from the table.

She tried to elude the feeling of being forty, of the months of her life skidded away on a row of pills. She shielded her eyes from the bone-faced reflection in the kitchen window, looking beyond it to the children: Janey and Marty on the swings, Roy crawling near them stuffing fistfuls of grass into his mouth. Her vision swayed in and out of time. When she stared too long at Janey's swinging sneakers, they turned into black patent Mary Janes, into shiny teenage boots, into housewife slippers.

Someone thought of ice cream and the children were in and around her legs again, touching her with their wet clothes; Isabel didn't want to dig her hand into the cold carton. "No ice cream. You didn't eat your dinner." Janey's siren cry started up as Isabel swung through the door into the living room. "Brian, would you put the kids to bed tonight?" He looked up from the campus newspaper. "Sure. Get them into their pajamas and I'll do the rest."

Janey was still wailing, though the plea changed from ice cream to staying up later. It was the end of the week, end of the clean laundry, the hamper overflowing. Isabel tossed through the drawers trying to find tops and bottoms of pajamas that were the right size for the right kid, and Janey objected that she didn't like those blue ones because they were too tight, and she was right, the wrist elastics cut her, but they were the only clean ones so Isabel searched for a scissors to cut the elastic, but then thought maybe she shouldn't; would they fit Marty next? All she could find was a small nail scissors. I've *got* to take a pill, she thought, walking out of the kids' room. Brian was still bending over the four-page newspaper.

"Brian. If I get them into their pajamas, what's the rest?"

"What do you mean?"

"I mean what are *you* going to do? Read them a story?"

"Yeah, I'll read them a story."

Her mouth hung open, drying in the air. "Why don't *you* get them into their pajamas!" The screen door banged as she stepped into the yard.

Chopper was waiting for Zimmie on the porch. He grinned as she plodded up the steps and read from his leather-bound Mao: "Investigation may be likened to the long months of pregnancy, and solving a problem to the day of birth. To investigate a problem is, indeed, to solve it." Zimmie paused before him, slowly shaking her head, then walked into the house, throwing her pocketbook towards the closet and slumping on the couch.

Chopper followed her in. "What happened today? Are they going to let us film the birth?"

"How was your day?" she mumbled, feeling too tired to talk.

"Not bad. I went to some classes and I played ball. It was a great game. I hit a double and they walked me twice and I stole second. Then I got home and put up the rice and took a shower and wondered what was taking you so long." He kept shaking out the length of his hair to dry it; we're a couple of mangy animals, Zimmie thought, feeling hot, fat, and beastly.

On her walk home she'd caught the last of the rain, then the return of the hot sun. She felt a slow anger smoking over the top of the volcano.

"I'm glad *you* had a nice day."

"You had a bummer. I can see you had a bummer."

She took off her sandals and threw them against the closet door. "If you want to film reality you should sit with me for four hours waiting for the damn doctor. That could be the climax of the film: at last, the doctor emerges from his hiding place, snatches a look at the patient, and quickly retreats. The patients shuffle back to their pens."

"Is everything o.k.?"

"Poke, poke, squeeze up your blood pressure, that's all, dear."

"Well, it won't be much longer. I remember at first you were so excited every time you got to go to the doctor."

"Was I?" She tried to remember that feeling but couldn't escape the present. "Instead of hassling myself about your stupid film, I should've figured out a way to ask him the real questions. Will my kid be healthy? Am I going to live through it? Why do I feel like crying all the time but never do? Man, I understand why in the old days women never left the house when they were pregnant. It makes me feel so . . . forlorn."

He sat down across from her, looking at the camel shape on the sofa. Zimmie struggled out of her dress, tossing it across the room. "I guess the end is the hardest part," he said finally. "You really had it together until this week. That's what gave me the inspiration for the video: not just the birth thing, but the way you were just grooving along with this incredible optimistic spirit."

"What are we having with the rice?"

"We got some vegetables in there. We can start cutting them up soon. Fuck, Zimmie, aren't you going to tell me what they finally said about the filming?"

The anger began to revive her. "You think you're gonna make the revolution shooting video tapes, don't you?"

"I never said that." His muscles tensed, arms clenched on hips.

"Well, I'm bored stiff of your film. All those hours I was thinking about it, all the way home I was wondering how you'd take it, and then I thought, this doesn't have a damn thing to do with me. Chopper's a nice guy and all, but . . ."

"What's with you? You were all excited about the film we made on the school system. You did a lot of work on that. I think we really showed how bored the kids are and how they're taught this patriotic and sexist stuff."

"You got an A for the film."

"So?"

"So what's it to me?"

"I don't buy that. Your name's on it. You can show it anywhere you want."

She kicked her feet against the arm of the couch until she could summon a reply. "You're the worse kind of pig—a pig wrapped in a red flag!"

He looked startled. With his face struggling between suppressed laughter and anger, he moved towards her, reaching to touch her hair, but she shook him off. "Look, Zimmie, I'd like to have a good discussion with you about this, but you're so irritable . . . Do you want me to run you a bath?"

She nodded, glaring at the floor until he left the room, then shouted, "And make me a joint."

"Fuck," he yelled from the bathroom, "you know there's none left. I've been meaning to talk to you. . . ." but as he reentered the room and saw her charging face he let his voice drift.

Zimmie stepped into the tub, worrying a little. Wasn't there something in the book Isabel had given her about not taking baths in the ninth month? The doctor hadn't mentioned anything. She relaxed in the water, watching her stom-

ach floating like an island in front of her. A pig in a red flag
—she grinned. That was the first time she ever called Chopper a pig. She stretched her arms above her head. He deserved
it, not only for today but for . . . she tried to force herself to
finish the thought, to face the image of Chopper and Ann
she'd been shoving under the rug of "jealousy is a selfish
emotion." She couldn't confront that conflict between her
need for freedom and her desire for some assurance that the
next time she turned around Chopper would still be there.

She hugged her stomach, trying to embrace the baby. It
was amazing that Chopper put up with her at all, she thought,
soaping slowly. He must be only part pig to nurture her
through a pregnancy he had no part in. But then it was amazing that she put up with him. All this talk about cameras and
taping while the real source of the race, the energy of creation, was right inside her, exerting a powerful gravity on her
being. Dr. Shote had made the whole idea sound so obscene, as
if all she wanted to do was spread her legs before a camera.
Zimmie slid carefully out of the tub. She wrapped a towel
around her midsection and walked towards the kitchen with
the water still dripping off her.

Chopper brought the cutting board, knife, and a sack of
vegetables to the table for Zimmie to slice. He attacked the
dishes in the sink with more noise than speed. After listening
to the clanging awhile, Zimmie asked, "How much of these
vegetables should I use?"

"All of them—I'm starved."

"Did you score any grass today? I could really use a
joint."

"Zimmie, I've been meaning . . ." He turned and laughed
at her expression. Her eyes were squinted shut as if she
expected the ceiling to fall. "I've been . . . How come you
smoked up all my dope while I was away? There were over
two ounces of grass there. What'd you do—have pot parties
every night?"

"No. I stayed home and smoked myself into a stupor."

"What was the point of that, you damn hippie?"

"Maybe you'd feel better if we shot a video tape about getting stoned."

He turned and flung a handful of water at her. "I'm glad we don't have any. This is the first decent confrontation we've had since I've been back. And that's the point of us living together, right?"

She chopped the carrots quickly, enjoying the sound of the knife knocking against the board. "I thought you loved me."

"I do. I love a lot of people. But the reason—"

"What do you talk to Ann about?"

"Oh, we have some good discussions. Mostly about relationships and sex roles and stuff."

"As long as we're having a confrontation, Chopper, I've been meaning to tell you that though I don't get jealous if you sleep out, I do get jealous watching Ann run her pretty fingers through your pretty yellow hair and watching your neck relax back into her hands and you both get those goo-goo expressions on your faces." Chopper's face flushed. "Now this may be my hang-up, but even when I was a kid I always managed to squeeze between Mom and Pop when they hugged in front of me. The other night I just barely kept myself from stomping on both of you."

Chopper had piled the dishes in a precarious mountain on top of the drainboard and was working on the wok with steel wool. "Were we doing that a lot?"

"Not a lot. But even once is a lot." She kept her eyes on the cucumber she was scraping the seeds out of and cutting in strips.

"O.k., I got you."

"What's that mean?"

"I accept the criticism. We won't make goo-goo faces in front of you anymore."

They regarded each other unsteadily, on the verge of

smiles. The exhaustion rolled off Zimmie and settled around her feet like puddles. "It's a relief to have that out. I didn't realize how much it was bothering me until just now when it stopped bothering me."

Chopper scraped the vegetables off the board into the wok, slowly stirring them about in the popping oil. "Well, what else is bothering you? We haven't been communicating very well. You haven't even asked me how my trip went, except in a real sarcastic way. I haven't even told you what happened when I went home."

She let the bath towel settle around her lap. The first evening breeze was coming through the screen window. "It's rough living with a privileged bastard like you. You get to go on vacations. You get to turn the scariest moment of my life into a television program. Whew. All right, tell me—what happened when you went home?"

He regarded her hesitantly, until she said, "Go on, go on, tell me the whole fascinating story."

"Well, I saw my parents. Every time I go home I see them in an entirely different light. You know I never told my father I lost my athletic scholarship on that free-music bust. I sort of hinted at it, but I never came out with it. So I told my mother last week, and then I went out to see some friends and I knew she'd tell my father, and when I got back he was waiting for me. That means he was asleep in the arm-chair with the sports page on his lap and the t.v. on and he woke up as I opened the door and took off his glasses and rubbed his eyes and motioned me to sit down. He mumbled a lot of things I didn't understand, but he wasn't as mad as I thought he'd be. It was as if he'd been hoping I'd make it but deep down he knew I'd fuck up. Finally he said, 'Well, there's always the hard way left,' and went to bed."

Zimmie laughed. "He sounds neat."

"I used to hate him. All the time I was growing up he'd push my mother around, shoving her into a chair during arguments. Ugh, I hated them both. Her for the way she jumped at everything he said as if she were touched by a cattle prod. They seemed so different this time, talking about retirement plans, hoping for the best for their only son but not expecting much."

He served out the vegetables and rice and sat down opposite Zimmie. "I told my mother about you. She says she's going to knit something for the kid."

"Really? Isn't it funny I never learned to knit? I thought it would just come automatically with pregnancy."

He shook his head. "You're not the knitting type."

"What type am I?"

"You'd like to know, wouldn't you? You'd like me to spend all my time telling you about yourself."

"Of course!"

"You're the dangerous-type girl. I'd hate to be the doctor that kept you waiting."

She laughed. "He told me I was the only patient who ever complained about it."

"Is it safe to ask now what's happening with the film?"

She ate a few mouthfuls, slowly. "My doctor said it was o.k. The head doctor said no, impossible, some guy bumped his head in the delivery room and sued the hospital for eighty thousand. So I asked Crinose to help, but we probably won't know until we get there."

Chopper began attacking the mounds of food on his plate, shaking on the soy sauce.

"I've been working on a new song," she said, pausing to remember it and enjoy the gray glimmer of interest in Chopper's eyes.

Are you a hippie or a radical?
There's a difference—that I know
Between fighting exploitation
And just digging the daily flow

Do you want to fight to change things?
Can you resist temptation
To space out in the country
Saying, I'll found my own nation

I'm a welfare mother, baby
That's a class reality
And it sure is different than playing
At the free university

You may like revolution
Because of the romance
But I need a revolution
Just to give my kid a chance

So tell me what's the answer
Help me find the way

"There's gonna be more—as soon as I figure it out."
He had finished eating; she shoved her plate towards him.
"You sure? You should eat more of this. You need to keep
your energy up."
"I'm too worn out. You eat it." He refused, but she
knew he'd soon take it.
"Your voice is getting a lot better, Zimmie. It sounds like
conversation and singing at the same time. I think I get what
you're saying. But what should I do? Quit school?"
"I don't know what you should do."
"Get a job in a factory and support you and the kid and
agitate?"
"I don't want to be supported. Don't look at me like you
think I've got some kind of secret plan."
"Well, hell, I don't want to get a job. I'd be buried before
my time." They laughed, their fingers touching between the
plates. "But you're raising something important."

6

The baby's kicking—
He's pleading with me
Mama mama I want to be free
Free me, free-ee me now

"Iz."
"Yes."
"I'm having them. I think it's them. But how can I time them if I don't get any pauses? Is this it?"
"Are you going to the hospital?"
"Just come over. See if you think this is it. If not, I've got something terribly wrong with my stomach."
Isabel decided to wear a dress and stockings, hoping to placate the doctors by looking respectable. Brian stood by, holding Roy, his mouth opening and closing like a fish as he started to speak to her dashing form, then shut his jaws before the sounds came out.
"Will you call and cancel my classes, Brian? There's some frozen pies for dinner."
"When this is all over, Isabel—"
"Janey, do you have Mommy's shoes again?" She shook her head no, grinning down at her feet. Isabel lifted her daughter out of the shoes.
"When this is all over . . ." Brian began. Isabel brushed her hair down briskly, but little tufts stuck out all around. "We can't just keep this up," he said from the doorway of the bathroom. "It's terrible . . . for my work."
"Your work—" Isabel shrugged. She kissed Roy, losing herself in his smooth plump cheek. "Janey, Zimmie is going to have her baby now and Mommy is going to help her."

"Is it a boy or a girl?" She was sitting by the bed putting on Isabel's slippers.

"We don't know yet."

"You mean it's knocking to come out and you don't know yet?" Isabel laughed, kissing her. She couldn't find Marty until Brian pulled him from under the crib, where he was poking a lollipop stick in an electric outlet. She kissed him as if she were leaving forever.

"I worry about you," Brian said.

The baby's jumping—
He's knocking his knee
Mama mama let me out of here please
Free me, free-ee me now

Zimmie was lying on the couch when Isabel burst in, her teacup eyes clinking together with excitement. She waited with her hand on Zimmie's stomach, which rose into a hard knot, twisted to untie itself, then collapsed, only to rise and twist again in thirty seconds.

"Wow, you're not getting any pauses. Does it hurt much?"

"I've never felt like this before . . . scared."

Isabel smoothed strands of hair off Zimmie's face. "It might be soon. Where's Chopper?"

"I think he spent the night with his friend Ann. The number's on the wall."

The bastard, Isabel thought as she dialed. She couldn't understand those two. He didn't sound apologetic; he thanked her for calling and said he'd meet them at the hospital.

The baby's twisting—
He's turning in me
Mama mama you're strangling me
Let me be free, free-ee me now

Isabel started Zimmie on light breathing in the car, counting out the rhythm. Zimmie kept her eyes fixed on Isabel. This woman had done it three times, this woman who'd never have the nerve to run a live bomb down a service road. Three times. Zimmie vowed she'd never do it again, not on her life.

"We should call your parents. Does Chopper have their number?"

"What for? My parents"—she interrupted to do some breathing—"the last time I saw my parents was the last time I was in the hospital. Oh, I couldn't take it again. I'll call them when it's over."

Isabel remembered her parents flying a thousand miles to stand in the corridor while she gave birth to Roy, and how foolish she felt it was, and how glad she was. "You know having a kid will change your attitude towards your parents. It makes a big difference—they'll pay attention to him and leave you alone. I think you . . ."

Zimmie was shaking her head vehemently. "The last time I saw my parents I woke up in the hospital with this terrible stomach ache. You see, I had swallowed a bottle of quinine to . . . you know . . ."

Isabel's eyes dashed from the road to Zimmie's face. "Quinine?"

"You heard the one about quinine for home abortions. You never heard it? Well Richard heard about it and got me a bottle and I drank a lot of the stuff in a friend's apartment, in the bathtub of all places, and woke up in the hospital with a rotten feeling in my stomach. I turned my head to the right and there was my mother perched on a chair like a canary with tight blond curls around her face. I thought, oh no, so I turned my head to the left and there was my father sitting on a chair with his heavy farmer's hands resting on his knees. . . ." She breathed impatiently. "I must have died, I thought. This must be hell: always having to face your parents with what you've done."

"You really haven't seen them since?"

"Oh, they call and bother me all the time. I can't deal with it. I haven't even told Chopper much about the quinine thing: that attitude of trying to get rid of the kid and myself has nothing to do with how I feel now." She took irregular chest breaths, and Isabel began to count, trying to get her back on rhythm.

"Someday I'll write a song about my parents," Zimmie said as soon as the contraction was over. There was a pileup of cars over the bridge and the car shook as it idled.

I'm such a disappointment to my parents
I never did a thing that's right

She gasped. "I can't even tell if that was one, or the baby just moved, or . . ."

"My parents," Zimmie was saying as they walked into the hospital. "It's not that they don't understand me. They do understand me. They just can't believe it. You see, my father got his farm during the Depression. He never actually owned the land; the bank owned it and the house, they repossessed it from someone and got my father to work it; the farm was run like a family farm except part of the profits went to the bank and we couldn't remodel the house or anything without . . ."

The admissions clerk was ready for them but Zimmie kept talking until Isabel poked her shoulder. Then she hurled information back at the clerk's questions. "Oh no, I think the contractions have gone away," she said. In the elevator she continued: "Then when my father got sick, the bank just consolidated the farm with some others they had and we had to move into town. Now he collects disability and drinks and broods around the house, while my mother got a job as a hairdresser in town. . . ." Her stomach twisted suddenly and she clutched the bar in the elevator.

Isabel waited in the corridor while the nurse prepared Zimmie, flattening herself against the wall to let the attendant jiggle by with his cart of prune juice and ice water, letting her mind bob on a flood of thoughts of her parents, Zimmie's parents, Brian's parents. Her parents' alarm when she told them she was pregnant for the third time, and her own hope for a miscarriage when she spotted blood early in her pregnancy after a violent fight with Brian in which she threw a cup of (cool) coffee in his face and he retaliated by spilling a carafe of (warm) coffee down her back, and she lay in a cold bath wondering at her madness at wanting another child. Three children was overdoing it, her mother said, why overdo it? Why? Why indeed? Why hadn't she become a gold-medal Olympic swimmer, and why, when Brian and she were tipping away from each other, did she insist on reenacting the maternal drama . . . Oh, don't torture yourself, Izzy, she chided, nothing you can do about it now. You've got three children . . . four counting Brian . . . You're doomed to make it work, either in this marriage or the next, it doesn't matter which.

She wandered down the hall to the nursery window, inspecting the newborns. None of them are mine, she thought, remembering how Janey had been splotched and scabby like that one, and Marty had been perfectly calm and beautiful, and Roy had been a fat delight to hold as he gulped down his bottles. Remembering the first moment the nurse left her alone with Roy when she wondered, Do I love you? and didn't have the answer yet. Next to Isabel a new grand-mother and father looked at a ten-pound baby: "All those clothes I knit," the grandmother said, "too small." Further down the window two pregnant women in bathrobes pointed to the infants.

"You cut your hair off!" Chopper was aiming the video camera at her. "What a terrible job." Isabel pivoted to show

him the back. "You look good," he said. "Your eyes look . . .
clear. What happened?"

Isabel shrugged. "Just sprucing up for the big event."

"You were on pills the last time I saw you," he persisted,
lowering the camera. "At least that's what Zimmie said."

"No more."

"No more. Never? I'm forever swearing off things
myself."

She shrugged again. "It's a renewable prescription."

His smile was so wide that she stepped away from it. "I'd
like to talk to you about it. Let's go drinking when it's all
over."

She nodded, leading him back down the corridor. Zimmie
opened the door for them. Chopper filmed the yellow room,
the stiff bed, the intravenous equipment.

"Don't you think we should call Zimmie's parents, Chopper? I don't mind doing it. Now that I know all about
them . . ."

"You don't know all about them," Zimmie said. "I never
finished my story."

"It's up to Zimmie," Chopper said. "She can call them
once the baby's born."

If something goes wrong, Isabel brooded, and I have to
explain to those people why we didn't call them earlier . . .

"You must think I hate my parents," Zimmie said, talking
fast between contractions, "but I don't. My father did some
neat things." She lay on the bed flipping her gown open so
Chopper could get a good shot of a contraction. Her face
was calm; she held onto Isabel's excited eyes and felt calm.
"My father hates the system as much as I do. During the
Depression he helped some other farmers move furniture
into a house during evictions—my mother helped too. They
always talked about the Phylox farm and how it was
never . . ."

A large-busted nurse entered the room and moved

towards Chopper, who had his camera trained on her. "Would you please come with me, sir?" He followed her down the corridor, filming her broad white backside. Isabel felt relieved to see him go.

". . . repossessed because the neighbors wouldn't allow it. Of course a lot of other farms in the area went under; that was just one case where they won. He didn't sympathize with . . ." She slowed down to take the long shallow breaths, then resumed, ". . . *me* though. He doesn't believe in terrorism or sabotage."

"Neither do I," said Isabel.

"Well, I don't believe in it as a general policy anymore. But it's an o.k. tactic. Sometimes you need it. What else could three underground characters do in Muskmelon, Iowa? Hold a peace vigil?"

Isabel encouraged Zimmie to get off the bed and move around. She tried several positions: standing against the wall, sitting in a chair, kneeling on the bed. When Dr. Crinose came in he found Zimmie sitting on the floor with her back against the wall delicately massaging her stomach. He drew the curtain around the bed. "You're dilated two," Isabel heard over the curtain rod.

"Doctor, if she's still in the first stage, how come she's having her contractions so close together?"

Dr. Crinose rubbed his beard. "The first stage of what?"

Isabel had a Lamaze manual in her hand: "It says the contractions come five minutes apart until—"

"Everything's fine," he said. "Don't worry about a thing."

"Everything's fine with you!" Zimmie yelled after him. "In here we're coming to grips with cosmic forces."

He stuck his head back into the doorway, grinning. "I'll check you in a couple of hours, Zimmie."

The strength of the contractions seemed to let up a bit once they realized how far from the end they were. Zimmie tried to talk right through the pain: "I wonder what the doc's first name is? Remind me to call him Charley next time he comes in."

They settled back on the floor. Isabel was reminded of a pajama party, the kind of female intimacy when girls set each other's hair and Isabel was taught to shave under her arms. Zimmie felt as though she were crouching on the side of the road with the bomb inside her this time. She could picture the coming birth as the flash of a star coming into being out of a black hole.

"I spoke to one of Brian's colleagues, a physicist, about black holes," Isabel said. "He thinks it's just a mathematical theory with no real proof. He said the reason scientists are writing about it in public journals has to do with the cutbacks in research money. They're trying to generate public excitement to get back their government grants."

Zimmie looked very sad. "I should have known it was another dead end. Chopper and I spent so much time figuring out that stuff and it still didn't help us make the revolution. But maybe Brian's friend is wrong."

The hours went by, marked by the regular metronome of the contractions. Isabel offered to read from a book of poems she'd brought along, but Zimmie shook that off. "Talk to me instead. You haven't called Brian all day, have you?"

"I'll see him later."

"How's it been going?"

"Worse and worse. I'm not taking the tranquilizers, so everything hurts more. But hell, if I have to pay for his mistress's abortion, he can put up with my moods."

"Whaaa . . . ?" Zimmie began, then switched into shallow panting as the contraction gathered force. Isabel stood over her, pressing her fists against Zimmie's back to relieve some of the pressure. She felt as if she had her hand on a huge turbine engine. Zimmie relaxed and groped for the bed, falling on her back. "Now, that was something."

"Don't stop breathing until the contraction is completely over," Isabel advised. "And you should start earlier too, as soon as you feel it start."

"What abortion? What mistress?"

"I guess that's why Brian stopped talking to me six months ago; he was afraid if he opened his mouth he'd spill the news of his love affair."

"Well, I don't believe in monogamy anyway, but it's a drag he made such a secret . . ."

Her stomach rumbled twice, then began to quake. The large muscular movement rippled through her. She panted quickly, trying to keep the ripple from reaching her brain. This was a strong one. She rubbed her stomach, turning on her side so Isabel could press her back. She reached back and pushed Isabel's fists further down to the root of the pain. She was panting. She kept panting until the feeling rippled out of her toes.

"That was a good one," Isabel said. "I think I should call the doctor."

Zimmie grabbed her arm. "Stay." Isabel sat back down on the bed. "I need you: you're so strong." Isabel flushed with power. When she was eleven she used to feel this strong and brave. She wiped Zimmie's forehead with a damp cloth as she lay sweating and tired on the stiff sheet. "You're the one who's strong. Not a complaint out of you. You're doing so well."

"Am I?" It was hard for her to realize that Isabel saw only her well-controlled relaxation, heard her correct breathing, but couldn't hear her mind, which was at every moment ready to cry out and break. Like after three days at the lie-detecting machine with her arm so sore in the pit from being strapped to the high table, her will so weakened by her father's arm around Sheriff Mantelface's shoulder.

The next contraction seized her with a sudden pinch.

She panted frantically. Fuck. Shit. Fuck this shit. This was the end. This was rotten. How could she ever love her child after this? How could she . . . it passed mercifully quicker than the others. "I think you showed a little blood," Isabel said. "I'll ring for the nurse. Try to relax your face next time. You looked like you were pushing over a mountain." She laughed, and her laughter sounded to Zimmie like a thousand glasses of wine clinking together in a white rose red splash.

A nurse ran in. Isabel showed her the blood on the now-wrinkled sheet. She put a paper diaper under Zimmie and explained she would call Dr. Crinose, who was napping in the residents' quarters. Zimmie kept her eyes closed now. She held Isabel's fingers tightly. When the doctor appeared he asked Isabel to wait outside and closed the door.

Zimmie was startled when she heard the door close. A fresh contraction began immediately and the nurse had her hand on Zimmie's mound. Dr. Crinose began his examination. Zimmie felt as if she were being torn apart by the hinges. A gush of water ran out of her. She stopped panting in surprise, and the full force of the rupture hit her brain. She heard someone scream, a deep long scream, full of fear.

Isabel was talking to Chopper, who had returned without his camera, when they heard the bellowing scream from behind the closed door. With a shudder they clung together, holding each other by the shoulders, silently waiting the long long minutes until the doctor opened the door. The nurse was folding back the screen. Zimmie was panting on the bed, her face purple. The doctor had reached in and broken her water without a warning. Isabel's face glowed over her. Chopper was stroking her hand. The next few contractions plunged Zimmie into despair. She was no hero. She'd never make it. What right had she to push herself so hard? She wondered what the Demerol waiting in the needle on the nurse's tray would do.

The baby's struggling—
To get out of me
Mama mama you're strangling me
I gotta get free, free-ee

Her lips formed the shape of the lyrics, but no sound came out.

The doctor came back to check her. This time he let Isabel and Chopper remain. "You're dilated nine," he said, removing dripping fingers. "If you want to push—"

It came like a seizure. She sprang up in the bed, sitting on her heels, holding onto the railing, pushing down with her pelvis, her stomach, her teeth, her rib cage, pushing way down; she felt the baby move way down as she struggled to dislodge her load.

Isabel's cool fingers touched her cheek. "Relax your face. Relax your arms. Relax your jaw."

The movement ended. The baby slipped way back up to her ribs. Zimmie fell on her back.

"I've done that before," she gasped. "Somewhere." Her brain struggled to recall the moment.

In each succeeding universe
Time flows in the opposite direction

Isabel wiped Zimmie's forehead with a towel. Chopper's face was lit up in adoration. "You pushed very well, like a champ," the nurse said.

In each succeeding universe
Time spins in the opposite . . .
Mommy mommy did you do this to me?

The next seizure was no less sensational. It consumed Zimmie. Her soul pushed down. Her cells pushed down. Her mind

was afloat among the body sensations . . . protesting slightly
. . . ow! . . . the more she pushed the less stress she felt. The
worst was waiting, blowing out hard, the ten seconds while
the contraction gathered strength. The pushing, oh, it was
something to do. The nurse ran for the doctor.

"Please don't bother with the delivery room; let her stay
here," Isabel asked.

On the next push the head showed. Isabel and Chopper
were hugging each other in excitement at the sight of the
brown hair. Zimmie's eyes were closed. She was too weak to
get up for the pushes. She remained on her back watching a
tiny black hole, far away among the nebulae, way down there,
opening up, giving birth to a universe.

She waited in a long spin, stilling herself to gather strength
for the next chance to push. She was being turned inside out.
The baby's head held her open like a jammed door. She was
giving birth to a giant, to the whole round globe of the earth.
When she began to push again the doctor cut to prevent a
tear.

With a squish the baby slipped out. All pressure ceased. It
was over. I feel fine, she thought, fine! The squish landed on
her stomach. She raised her head and saw a blue coiled cord
attached to a skinny infant. The cord fascinated her. It was
thick, spiraling with blue blood. She let her head fall back.

"Look at this," Dr. Crinose said. He opened the infant's
fist. She was clutching an IUD.

The next time Zimmie opened her eyes the baby was next
to her, wrapped tight as an outgoing sandwich in a white
receiving blanket. Her purple eyes, like lights down the end
of a telescope, fastened on her mama. "Welcome to the universe," Zimmie said. The purple lights blinked. They popped
the baby into a plastic rectangle.

"Is that an incubator?" Zimmie asked. No one answered
her. Chopper pocketed the IUD for a keepsake.

"Give me another one of those good pushes now," the doctor said.

"Is that an incubator?" Zimmie yelled. She'd be damned if she'd push again. The doctor leaned on her stomach to deliver the afterbirth. Zimmie pulled on Isabel's arm. "How come she's in an incubator?"

"No, that's the crib thing they put them in. She's a good size."

"I thought she looked small." Zimmie heard herself say "she." A girl . . . oh hell . . . does that mean I'll have to become a feminist?

7

"Rosa Luxemburg Alp," Zimmie decided. Chopper leaped in approval. Isabel wondered who Rosa Luxemburg was. Zimmie was lying on her stomach facing out into the recovery room. Her face was mottled with tiny broken blood vessels. Her body felt limber and fit. She was puzzled by this wait for "recovery." Surely she could have danced away from the delivery room. The other patients were surrounded by curtains, still unconscious from their births.

Isabel was stretched back in a chair, her nylons scraping the backs of her knees. She held Zimmie's hand. She felt totally satisfied: she'd been there; she'd helped; the steel point of ecstasy had touched her heart.

"Where's your camera?" Zimmie asked Chopper.

His face darkened. "I would have punched that guy, but I didn't think you'd appreciate a hospital riot today. I had this image of Dr. Shote running down the hall with his nose bleeding and his glasses broken while I set fire to the medical journals in his office. 'I have a son just like you,' he said. 'Thinks he can do what he damn pleases. I'm in charge of this hospital. I worked hard for this position.' He set it up so I had to choose between leaving my camera or leaving the hospital."

Zimmie shook her head. "Anyway, you saw her being born with your own eyes instead of through a lens. We'll never forget . . ." But she worried as she tried to snatch at the day. The memory of the pain, the pushing, the opening up, eluded her. Could it fade that quickly? All that remained was the relief and a vigorous energy in her muscles.

"It was the most amazing thing I've ever seen," Chopper said. "And your face, Zimmie, it was so impressive: red as a brick wall, concentrated and relaxed. I've never seen anything like it."

Zimmie rolled over on her back, then flopped onto her stomach again, twisting the sheets. "I feel so good."

"Do you have clothes to bring the baby home in?" Isabel asked.

Zimmie shrugged. "Those things you gave me . . . some things I took from Boomer's last week."

Chopper feigned a punch at her. "I thought we swore off . . ."

"Come on, you know I never steal more than I can wear. But now I'll have two backs to cover."

Their laughter stirred the woman in the next bed. "Is it over yet?" she called out.

"You bet it is!" Zimmie answered. "Aren't you glad?" She turned to Isabel. "I guess I've done everything now. Only death will be a new experience."

Isabel shivered. "I thought I was falling into that black

hole the other day. But you haven't done everything. You haven't even held your baby yet."

A nurse came to check the patients and invited Isabel and Chopper to leave. Visiting hours were over. They covered Zimmie's bloodshot cheeks with kisses. They stopped at the nursery window, but Rosa hadn't checked in yet. It was after eleven o'clock, they realized with surprise, as they stepped into the night.

As soon as she was alone, Zimmie pulled up her hospital gown and studied her stomach. It was still rounded, with flaps of slack skin curling around her waist. She slapped away at it, smiling at her freedom, at the regained sense of privacy; her body was all hers again; the intruder was gone. As soon as she got home she planned to play rock records and dance around the living room until she gyrated back to her normal weight. How do you feel? I feel fine! she kept thinking, fine! The doctor had given her a shot of novocaine before stitching her up, and she thought of feeling around for the stitches but found her interest in the gory details of birth had passed. She pulled down her gown and swung her legs over the side of the bed. A passing nurse shook her finger at her and told her to lie down. "Can I get something to eat?" Zimmie asked. "How about a steak, french fries, and a Coke?" The nurse laughed and brought her a paper cup of grapefruit juice and a cookie she'd saved from her own lunch.

I'll have to tell Chopper to bring my blue jeans, Zimmie thought. Her eyes roamed around the recovery room, but there was nothing in the soundproofed ceiling, utility tables, and bedsteads to hold her eye. I'll get Chopper to bring that Indian madras bedspread and hang it up for me to look at. And some books . . . I'll need something to do if I'm going to be here four days.

Then she remembered about the baby. She had requested rooming-in so that the infant would get the full benefit of her attention. The baby . . . She looked like a stranger, Zimmie thought with alarm. I've never seen her before in my life; she's a total stranger. Somehow she'd expected to recognize the baby immediately, to think, oh of course, this is the baby, the one I'm supposed to have, the one I've been lugging around all these months. Instead she'd be taking an alien with purple eyes home with her.

Zimmie thought about getting into blue jeans again and dancing around the living room with Rosa (would that name be all right?), Rosa hanging in the sling Isabel had given her, or in the baby carrier Zimmie intended to swipe from Boomer's.

It was more than an hour before two male attendants came to wheel her into her own room. As they were moving down the corridor, Zimmie asked them to stop by the nursery window. She started to read the name cards attached to the cribs when her eyes lit on Rosa. That looks just like her. She read "Alp" on the card. Of course, that's her, I recognized her! she thought with joy. None of the others looked anything like that baby with her diamond-shaped cheeks and thin black hair. Even with her purple eyes squinted closed, Zimmie recognized the face. She's still a stranger, Zimmie thought, glancing into the darkened rooms as they rolled down the hall, but at least I remembered her face.

Sitting in the back booth of the bar, Isabel studied Chopper. His flannel shirt was torn from the elbow to the cuff. The orange plaid flamed red and brown at the edges. His light hair was parted widely in the center and pulled back into a ponytail. He had a long M-shaped mustache. Isabel thought he smiled and laughed a lot for a man. It was so easy to be male. They never knew what it was like, rock scraping rock for unending time, pelvic bone crushing against skull bone. Isabel's sides still ached in identity with Zimmie's labor pains. Her elbows were damp against the Formica table.

"O.k., maybe men have it easier," Chopper said. "But at

least Rosa won't feel she has to pitch a no-hitter to be a real man. And with a mama like Zimmie, she's not likely to be a cheerleader either. Isn't Zimmie great? I bet she could raise ten kids by herself and still have time to run the revolution."

Isabel fingered her beer. "Don't you consider yourself the daddy?"

"Me? Well, as long as I live with Zimmie I'll help take care of the kid—she'll make me. But we didn't plan this child together. When I met Zimmie she was five months pregnant and being bailed out of jail by a furious boyfriend who left her on the courthouse steps. 'You coulda got me busted, you bitch!' 'That's a lousy way to treat me,' she screamed back, 'after all I been through. You think it was fun sitting on that cold cement?' He was gone by that time and I was just coming out of court myself after paying a hundred-dollar fine for gate-crashing a concert, chanting Free Music for Free People, and she just continued the conversation with me. 'The sweater I took was over fifty bucks so the charge is grand larceny. Now I figure I won't do time, but with my record you never know when some judge will decide to teach me a lesson.' She really intrigued me. A bad girl. A rebel girl. A girl with a record. I went back with her to the commune she was living on at the time. Then we lived in a one-room cellar apartment until we found the house. She thinks Rosa is Richard's baby. Do you know him?"

"No."

"Anyway, she decided to be the mama/papa. We don't have any heavy commitments. We're both sexual anarchists: we want to have close relationships with as many people as possible."

"With you a bit more anarchistic than she," Isabel said. She found his attitude intolerable. Didn't he realize that the baby was going to need years and years of care?

"You mean I sleep around more?" His gunbarrel eyes were focused dead on her. "For one thing, I haven't been pregnant. And it's easier for me. So many women would like to have a nonsexist lover like me." Isabel watched his mustache rise and fall as he spoke. "I'm not a playboy and I'm not a jock but I love sex and sports. It's very hard to explain."

"I'll bet it is," Isabel said, standing up. She walked down the row of booths to the telephone, dialing her home number. She knew she'd let her hostility to Chopper come through. They were all alike. If not . . . There's a dangerous thought. If they weren't all alike, why was she stuck with Brian?

She told Brian all about the birth, asked about the kids, and listened to the details of his day. They chatted a long time. "But where are you now?" he said finally.

"I'm out celebrating."

"Are you coming home?"

"Yes, eventually. You go on to bed."

"I've got a surprise for you," he said. "My mom called tonight. She wanted to send us some kind of a present, so I suggested a plane ticket to New York for you and the kids. You could use a vacation after all the recent shocks. And a professional haircut." He laughed.

"A vacation with the kids?"

"Well. I didn't think you'd want to leave them."

"I think it would be better," Isabel said slowly, "for you and I to go away without the kids for a couple of days. We have to begin working some things out, or . . ."

"What do you mean? What do you want?"

"I think I want to run my own life."

"Ach—you do anyway, you run mine too. I never stopped you from doing anything you wanted to do."

Isabel sighed. "There's someone waiting for the phone, Brian. I'll be seeing you."

When she came back to the booth a couple of men sat across the table from Chopper, so she squeaked her thighs along the vinyl seat beside him. Thigh against thigh, his knee higher than hers, free-dangling calves bumping at the ankle bone. She started to pull away, but her leg didn't listen. Words flashed between Chopper and the men. She heard nothing but her brain telling her leg to move and felt her leg still leaning against his jeans in the cool draft under the table. Chopper was talking, his arms moving, describing a pitch. He moved his leg away. After a while the men went back to the bar. The waiter brought another pitcher of beer to the table.

"What did Brian have to say?" Chopper asked.

After a halting start, Isabel began to talk freely, dropping one by one the screens she had propped up between herself and her difficulties. Used to finding her revelations hurled back at her off the trampoline of Brian's criticism, she was glad to find that Chopper at least appeared to absorb what she said. He didn't feel it with her the way Zimmie did, but at least he chewed on it, considered it, seemed pleased that she was telling him.

She confessed her fear at the burst of newness in herself which threatened to destroy four lives for the sake of one, and the difficulty of expressing herself to Brian. She couldn't let her marriage fail, but it was no longer possible to avoid confrontations. She hated to argue with Brian because she couldn't tell whether it was better to win or lose. At least if she capitulated he was happy and they had a few days of peace. If he gave in he started a fight on another topic immediately to assert his supremacy. And the children: if she left Brian she'd have to leave the kids too; she couldn't handle them by herself. And she couldn't leave the kids. She wound herself into several tight circles, concluding miserably that there was no solution.

Chopper said it was all political, it was ridiculous to blame herself and Brian as if they were the only two forces on earth. But there had to be a solution.

Isabel shrugged. "I'm sort of apolitical."

"You are or Brian is?" Chopper said. "I mean politics in the sense of taking power over your own life."

The word politics made Isabel shrug: she didn't understand it. Who's Rosa Luxemburg? she asked, and Chopper explained she was a German communist leader, a friend of Lenin's. He told her about a summer he spent on an assembly line working in a nail factory, watching the wire drawn through the die, and the machine cutting off pieces, stamping a head on each nail, trying to relate to the workers who spoke Spanish, Serbo-Croatian, and Haitian French, except for the commonality of American curse words. At the end of the line, checking the machine that packed the nails into boxes, was an old Hungarian. The shift started at seven in the morning and around nine thirty the first day the Hungarian stopped work and yelled out: "O.k., boys, we've earned our pay, the rest of the day we work for the boss." He had been on the job fifteen years and figured out exactly how many nails times the market price equalled his pay. From nine thirty to four p.m. Chopper felt like a slave. "I got real political that day."

The bartender moved from booth to booth. "Last call."

"Well, what are you going to do, Isabel? Go home to Brian or come home with me?" The flames on his flannel shirt leaped. He was smiling. "You're thinking, they're all alike, so what does it matter? Come home with me and we can talk some more and then I'll take off my clothes and you can do whatever you want to me."

He got up to get a six-pack from the bar, leaving her to wonder what she would do with the opportunity. To make him lie still and let me go as slowly as I want over his bumpy chest, around the bicep, just playing. To let the passion rise of its own accord, not by a set plan. She thought of Zimmie sprawled back, the globs of blue and stringy flesh.

"Zimmie wouldn't mind," he said. "It was practically her suggestion."

"Brian would." Zimmie wouldn't mind, but Brian would. Would she or wouldn't she? Small talk, she thought; the drama fled quickly.

"It seems like we should be able to love more than one person without hurting anyone—but I don't know. The truth is that no one is monogamous," Chopper said.

Isabel began to fidget. What is the act of love? Body on body, no matter how long, it always seems brief. Chopper looked a little bored, too. Something in the atmosphere. She turned and saw the bartender pushing a broad broom along the booths. "Closing."

"Let's go throw some rocks at Zimmie's window," Chopper said. "I think I figured out which side her room is on. She's probably awake with excitement—"

"Asleep with exhaustion."

"Let's do it! You've got the car."

She felt relieved that his thoughts were on Zimmie rather than her. She almost gave him the keys to drive—it's your idea; I'm not responsible—but what would she do then, just sit back and brood? She drove towards the hospital through the empty small-town streets with a string of red lights. It was ridiculous, not just her own timidity, she realized as they stumbled on the wet grass, dampening their shoes.

"Zimmmmmieeee," he yelled up the brick wall.

A shade snapped up. "Oh, you maniacs! But I can't escape, there's screens on the window."

"We're so excited!" Chopper was leaping towards the second story. They're kids, Isabel thought; she expects him to do things like this. What am I doing here?

"How ya feeling?"

"Perfect! Celestial!"

She'll know we're going to make love, Isabel thought.

"I just fed her. She sucks so hard, her jaws work like a little pig." Zimmie scratched and tapped musically on the window screen:

"Rosa Lux, oh Rosa Lux
Your purple eyes are glorious
Your destiny is clear to see
You'll fight forever for . . .

something or other. Say, Iz, are you sure they're going to let
me keep her? I keep expecting the nurse to say, 'You incom-
petent hippie, give me that baby, I'll find a respectable home
for her.' "

"Don't worry," Isabel whispered hoarsely. "You're stuck.
No one else wants her." Was she dreaming this moonlight on
the grass? Was she really home sleeping?

"Isn't it wonderful?" Zimmie was shouting. "Even under
this rotten capitalist system mothers have a right to their own
children. What'll they think of next?" Faces appeared at vari-
ous windows along the yellow wall. *Shhh.*

"Did you call your parents?" Isabel asked.

"Uh-huh. They're coming down tomorrow."

Chopper hugged Isabel all the way back to the car, the
way she'd seen him hug Zimmie, big-armed embraces that
lifted her heels off the ground. "Isn't she terrific? Confused
as hell, but in just the right way."

Isabel started the car. "Where to?"

Chopper let his orange plaid shoulders rise and fall. "I
think it's important to give women a chance to be aggressive
and make the decisions."

"I guess that means me." She felt stupid as she said it.

"Well, yeah"—he laughed—"I guess it does."

Isabel drove slowly back across Candle City, grateful for
every red light. In the back seat Zimmie was making wisecracks. Next to her sat Brian's headless mistress. Judy and
Brian were making love on the handlebars of the Harley-
Davidson that roared past the car. She heard children crying.
Surely this is an insignificant moment. When they reached
the house the apparitions vanished. Next to her in the dark

sat a single person she didn't want to say goodbye to. His foot jerked. Nervous, she thought with a smile, realizing he too must have been caught in a roar of thoughts during the silent drive. She turned off the motor and followed him inside the house.

They sat on the scratchy couch in the dark house drinking more beer. "Sometimes I like to get so drunk that the next day I have no memory of the hours before I passed out," Chopper said. "The no-memory zone: anything could have happened. I could have been a hero." He told Isabel about his childhood in St. Louis, the only son whose father spent long weekends training him to play ball, and how even now he found his purest satisfaction in the sweaty exertion, working closely with his team and against the others.

Isabel realized with a glow that he wasn't going to suddenly grab her in his arms. He would wait, talk, drink, shrug it off if they never touched. She reached out and pulled the hairband off his ponytail, loosening his long milkweed hair.

Impulsiveness, love of brawling, lack of ideology, those were his faults, he told her, and Zimmie's too. If they could only aim their energy straight at the temples of the ruling class, before they shot.

Isabel looked at him, enjoying the murmur of his talk, lightly touching his hair. It seemed like a long time before he fell silent. She wanted it to feel like a long time without lowering her glance, looking at his hair, looking at his fire shirt dancing colors in the dark until he said it burned him and took it off. She laughed, knowing he wasn't going to leap on her, and enjoyed the relief of rolling the scratching nylons off her legs. She didn't have to look away, to shield her eyes from him. She pulled her dress up over her head, unconscious of herself, falling into his eyes aimed at her like gunbarrels: hollow, gray, metal-colored, loaded. She touched his hand. They lay sideways on the floor, his gold erection rising to form a bridge between them. She drew closer until with a loud groan they disappeared into each other, tumbling, bumping, groping for the strongest contact, until they began the tremble towards orgasm.

Chopper rolled onto his back, pulling Isabel with him; she rested with her head on his shoulder, her lips on his neck, her fingertips massaging his scalp in moving circles. "Um. Feels good," he said.

When the rug began to itch under him, they moved unsteadily to Chopper's bed, shoving off the debris. He pulled at the jagged points of her hair. "You know, Isabel, I wasn't attracted to you until you cut your hair. And you had really beautiful hair."

She smiled in the dark, her fingers still moving over his body. "I wasn't attracted to you until you said you'd take off your clothes and let me do whatever I want."

He nodded. "It must be tough to be a woman. So much suspense—waiting to be seduced. I about collapsed from the tension."

He kissed her sluggishly on the lips, then folded a pillow under his head, "Big day," and fell asleep. Isabel wriggled on the creased sheet, trying to find a comfortable spot between the poking springs. She wanted to check on the children as she did every night, standing a moment in the warm darkness of their room growing sleepy gazing at their small faces. She tried to cuddle close to Chopper, but it was impossible. His foot twitched as he slept. She missed the easy postures she and Brian took in their sleep, as graceful and smooth as practiced dancing partners. She folded the other pillow under her head and fell asleep.

He was up before her in the morning, found her clothes, and laid them neatly by the bed. He made coffee. "Do you want to shoot a few baskets?" he asked. Did she! But not at the city recreation center; she'd run into everyone she worked with. And at the university gym they might see Brian's professors. She felt sulky, shading her tired eyes from the bright sunlight. Every move was such a big decision. Isabel always said she hated to make decisions, and Brian thought that was cute.

They went to the city rec center, where Isabel had gym shorts in her locker. The gym was empty except for an older man working out on an exercise machine. Isabel was good at shooting baskets from any standing position, but she'd never played competitive ball, so Chopper easily took the ball away from her. He was good at running shots, leaping shots. They played for an hour, coming closer in the sweaty crashing and rubbing of bodies than they had the night before. She thought him a good player. He said she was skilled, a natural, but lacking in fight.

In the pool she impressed him with her first racing dive, fancy underwater turning, swimming lap after lap of crawl, butterfly, breast stroke, back stroke. When she was finished thrilling her body by top performance, they swam slowly, watching each other through the splashes.

Zimmie was sitting up in bed. Her breasts were engorged, a word she'd just learned to explain the skin-bursting feeling that prevented her from lying on her stomach. She'd complained to the night nurse, who brought her plastic gloves filled with ice to put on her breasts. This hurt so much that Zimmie tossed them aside. The day nurse looked at the water-filled gloves in horror. "What you need is hot showers. Ice will stop the milk from forming." Zimmie related the whole thing to Isabel, sitting in the same clothes as yesterday, who said the only thing to do for engorgement was survive it; it only lasted a couple of days.

"I was with Chopper last night," she said at the first opening.

"Yeah, he called me this morning. He wanted to be the one to tell me. Said you swim a mean butterfly. Well, how was it?"

"Oh fine. Great, actually. My hair didn't get caught under me and twist my neck off. We had a great swim. How do you feel about it?"

Zimmie met her gaze and tried to let her see in. "Sometimes I miss Chopper when he's in the same room. It hurts to share, sometimes. But it's worth it." Tiny dots of sweat appeared on her blotched face. "There are these terrific compensations. Feeling really close to him, knowing we're together out of pure choice—not habit! not promises! not a structure! Hell, you don't expect Brian to be satisfied just talking to one other person. Why should he be satisfied with just one sexual relationship? Why should you?"

Isabel was sitting with her hands folded in her lap, listening intensely, trying to hear beyond the words. It was one thing getting lifted up by the gush of power from making her own decisions, and another thing wading through the results. "The truth is, Zimmie, you're the one I love."

Zimmie stretched her arms forward, smiling, then winced as her breasts rubbed together. "Are you going to go back to Brian?"

"I'm trying to think of one good reason to."

"Maybe you could talk him into giving any money he makes off those tales back to the Indians."

Isabel grinned. "Maybe."

"You were wonderful yesterday. You helped me more than I ever thought one person could help another."

They walked down the corridor together to the nursery. Rosa Luxemburg Alp was sleeping with a most adult expression on her face. "What's she dreaming about?" Zimmie wondered.

Isabel walked the blocks from the hospital to the house so quickly that she was flushed and panting when she arrived. The children caught her by the knees with a tumble of stories about making a puppet show with daddy and eating blue oatmeal. Brian chimed in, saying that Marty had yelled "Good idea, Daddy!" at his every suggestion, and it had been fun until lunchtime, when they refused to eat the soup he cooked because it had celery in it, and Roy dumped the bowl on the floor, and he wondered how Isabel put up with it. "There must be a natural mother instinct," he concluded.

It was the longest period of time Isabel had ever spent away from the children. She had missed them only briefly, but now she was glad to see their clowning faces. She decided the thing she resented most about Brian's love affair was his leisure; she would love to have several hours a day to spend with the adult of her choice.

Brian led her to the bedroom, gathering her closer and closer. Her main thought was to get out of her wrinkled clothes. "We're going to make it o.k. now," he said, pressing her damp head against his chest. "The abortion's taken care of, your nutty girlfriend has had her baby. Uphill from here, honey."

Isabel pulled away, stripping off her clothes. "Uphill? Uphill and pedaling all the way, I think. I'd like to take a nap."

"What about the kids?"

"What *about* the kids?"

Zimmie had finished feeding Rosa, wrapped her in the receiving blanket as the nurse had shown her, and put her back in the cubicle. The baby began to cry. The sound was like a signal from another planet. It made Zimmie jump. Eerie, she thought. She picked the baby up and felt her diaper. It was slightly damp, so she went through the exercise of pinning a dry, bulky diaper on her thin frame, stabbing her thumb with the diaper pin, trying to be calm, though the baby's wail was painful on the back of her neck. She held Rosa close to her chest, held her up in the air, jiggled her, even turned her upside down, but the crying didn't stop. She loosened the

receiving blanket, freeing the baby's arms and legs. Zimmie
was amazed at the agony the crying was causing her.

> I'm an odd sort of woman
> Coming home from a long exile
> An accidental mama
> Trying to court an infant's smile

Rosa stopped crying. Her fingers moved through the air like
tiny probes.

> There's a warm warm feeling
> Rushing through my body now
> There's a sweet milk feeling
> Ayee—Rosa's got a silly smile

Her purple eyes were wide open. She likes my singing, Zimmie thought.

> This women's revolution
> Has got a very subtle side
> It's yet to be unscrambled
> But we feel it very deep inside

Rosa's eyelids closed, fluttered, closed.

> In each succeeding universe
> You'll find a person just like me
> Trying to hasten the explosion
> See what the next change is gonna be.

Not a bad kid, Zimmie thought, placing her slowly in the
crib.

A Note on the Type

This book was set on the Linotype in Janson, a
recutting made direct from type cast from matrices
long thought to have been made by the Dutchman
Anton Janson, who was a practicing type founder
in Leipzig during the years 1668–87. However, it
has been conclusively demonstrated that these types
are actually the work of Nicholas Kis (1650–1702),
a Hungarian, who most probably learned his trade from
the master Dutch type founder Dirk Voskens. The
type is an excellent example of the influential and
sturdy Dutch types that prevailed in England up to
the time William Caslon developed his own incomparable
designs from these Dutch faces.

*Composed by Maryland Linotype Composition
Company, Inc.
Printed and bound by The Colonial Press,
Clinton, Massachusetts. Typography and binding
design by Susan Mitchell.*